Also available

Miss Understanding:
My Year in Agony

Miss Understanding

She tells it like it is

My Summer on the Shelf

Hodder
Children's
Books

A division of Hachette Children's Books

A Catalogue record for this book is available from the British Library

ISBN 978 0 340 98883 1

Typeset in Berkeley by Avon DataSet Ltd,
Bidford on Avon, Warwickshire

Printed and bound in Great Britain by
CPI Bookmarque Ltd, Croydon, Surrey

The paper and board used in this paperback by Hodder Children's Books
are natural recyclable products made from wood grown in
sustainable forests. The manufacturing processes conform to the
environmental regulations of the country of origin.

Hodder Children's Books
A division of Hachette Children's Books
338 Euston Road, London NW1 3BH
An Hachette UK company
www.hachette.co.uk

For Ella, Tilly and Theo

Email from Anya to Al – Monday 12th July 2010

Hey you

What do you think of this?

Al leaned forward, perhaps a little tentatively and our lips met. He's a good kisser, is Al. Especially when he's distracted by something. Maybe when I've just said something to throw him off balance. Like maybe I've just told him I think he's really sweet and that I'm really going to miss him, which is possibly the nicest thing I've ever said to him. I know that as a 'significant other' I can be a little sub-prime sometimes. But I think he quite likes me anyway.

It was a lovely kiss and I can still feel the tingle of his lips on mine. And even though he's going off to South America without me, I'm still happy.

Hey, don't get all 'Anya!' on me, OK? I'm not going to put that bit on the blog. That's just between you and me. I hope you have a good flight; I'm emailing this from the departure hall. I can't face getting back on the Tube just now so I'm having a coffee. You're just on the other side of that blank wall over there, probably being recruited by a Colombian drug smuggler named Fernando.

When you come back from Bogotá, remember don't agree to take any plastic bags full of 'icing sugar' through customs, OK? And it's not just drug smuggling you need to worry about. Keep your eye on your hand luggage or else someone will stuff half a dozen doped-up parakeets under your copy of *National Geographic*. How I wish I was going with you, you're going to have a great time. I, on the other hand, face a summer of trying to get Marley to eat something with vitamin C in it, and trying to get Mum to drink something without alcohol in it, all the time avoiding having to get a summer job. Mum's already started making worrying noises of that kind, and last night her boyfriend Lance (the Welsh plumber) asked me if I knew how to unblock a sink, which is not a question you want to hear from anyone, ever. Much as I like Lance, I do not want to spend the summer as his apprentice nozzle-fitter or trainee pipe-girl, or whatever they're called. What would we chat about? I've already exhausted my plumbing small talk with Lance.

'Did you know,' I asked him, 'that the flushing toilet was invented by a man named Thomas Crapper?'

'That's a common misconception, see Anya,' he said

regretfully. 'The flushing toilet was invented before Thomas Crapper was born.'

'So what did Thomas Crapper invent?' I asked.

'He invented the ballcock,' Lance said.

I stared back at him, evenly. 'Well, where are the comic possibilities in *that*?' I asked. I guess plumbing's not for me.

And look, about the other thing we were talking about. I know I've been blowing a little hot and cold. I really do like you, you know that. It's just that I'm nervous about starting a full-blown, holding-hands-in-the-corridors sort of relationship. I think that once you told me you were going away for the summer I just figured it was best if we wait and see how it all pans out. Eight weeks is a long time. Sorry for being so non-committal and I fully understand if you run off with some Dusky Latina and never come back to your Pale English Rose.

Sigh, I've depressed myself now. Might buy a choc muffin to keep me company on the train. See you in September!

Anya

Miss Understanding Blog Entry – 14th July 2010

Right! I'm back, and I'm madder than hell.

I know I said I was going to take a break from the whole blog thing but I didn't realize how much I'd miss venting my spleen on the internet. It's been a month since my last entry and my unvented spleen is now twice the size of Kanye West's ego.

Having said that, and before we go any further, let me get a few ground rules established.

1) There will be NO MORE advice dispensed on this website. I thought I'd made that perfectly clear back in June. It's totally over for me and the advice thing. But to judge by the number of emails I've received asking me how to hide love bites (use a scarf) or whether you should let Guy DuLancey take you ten-pin bowling on a first date (yes, but don't let him corner you behind the shoe-hire desk) it seems some of you didn't get the message. I'm

done with telling people how to behave, so stop asking!

2) I am only writing this blog as a way of getting me through the summer until school starts again. Al's in South America, pretending to be Bear Grylls. Mum and Marley are doing my head in. I can't go and stay with Dad because of my falling-out with Cheryl, so I need some means of escape.

3) As always all names are fictional and some events have been slightly rewritten to make me look cleverer and wittier than I probably appeared at the time. Also, some of the people portrayed in the blog may not actually be quite so stupid and/or irritating as I make them seem. I get a lot of emails from people accusing me of making everything up. Believe me or not, everything I write about on this blog actually happens for real, I might embellish things a little from time to time, but no more than that.

So what's driven me back to the laptop? OK, how about this for starters; yesterday my little brother Marley had his seventh birthday party. Preparations have been going on for some time, I found Mum looking through a Hamley's catalogue three weeks ago.

'If you spend sixty-five quid on Harry Potter merchandise,' she said, 'you get a free Invisibility Cloak.'

'Do we have sixty-five quid?' I asked. 'You told me the other day you were struggling to make the mortgage payments and therefore couldn't afford to buy me cheesecake any more.'

'Marley loves Harry Potter,' she said, peering at me in irritation.

'Oh well,' I said, shrugging. 'I suppose we can hide under the Invisibility Cloak when the bailiffs come round.'

On the day of the party, I blew up so many balloons I started to go a bit funny from oxygen deprivation and became convinced R. Kelly was hiding in the cupboard. I don't know how many of Marley's little bratpals turned up – a thousand perhaps? There was certainly a long string of tired nannies hurling small boys over the front fence all morning before dashing back to their SUVs. Within ten minutes of the arrival of the first guest all the balloons were popped, I had half a tube of Pringles down my top and a white marshmallow in my hair.

I was in charge of games and Jocasta did the food. I'd casually agreed to this back in June whilst distracted by a climactic scene in *Home and Away*. Only too late did I realize I'd drawn the short straw. I had to organize Pin the Tail on the Donkey (drawing pins hurt when they go into your thigh). Blind Man's Bluff (little boys' heads hurt when they ram into your stomach) and Pass the Parcel (parcel tape hurts when it gets tangled in your hair).

All my mother did was bring out the odd tray of veggie sausage rolls then hide in the kitchen with a cask of

Australian white wine. Not before she'd put on one of her old LPs. 'To get the party started.'

'What is this old crap you've put on?' I asked.

She peered at the record sleeve. '*Now That's What I Call Music! – Four*,' she read.

After an hour of this hell I plugged in the Nintendo to keep them occupied and snuck off to the loo for a quick nervous breakdown. Even there I didn't get any peace and quiet. I could hear them scuffling about outside grunting and trying to look through the keyhole. I felt like Sigourney Weaver in *Aliens*. Later Marley got stuck into the groaning table-full of presents and opened them in ten seconds flat. We'd got him some new games for his XBox and Mum got him a totally inappropriate box-set of gore-filled DVDs including *Hellslaughter Freak III* and *Serial Killer IV – Torture in the Toolshed*.

'That's more like it,' he said, inspecting the case for *Saw V – Uncut*.

'What do you mean?' Mum asked, limply holding a garbage bag while I shoved armfuls of shredded crepe paper into it.

'Well you didn't get me *anything* at Christmas,' he sniffed.

'What are you talking about?' Mum said. 'You got loads of presents this Christmas.'

'Yeah, from *Santa*!' he pointed out. 'Nothing from *you*.'

If it was just the one day I'd be all right with it but he's just so bored and so stuffed with energy these days it's like living with a manic depressive. He lies about on the sofa all day watching cartoons, then wakes me in the middle of the night asking for a sandwich, or for help destroying the giant floating eye thing in *Unreal Tournament: Mission Reloaded*. I love Marley to bits but he's just doing my head in right now. I need a break.

Mum's no better, you'd think she'd be grateful that I came back to live with her rather than Dad and Cheryl, but if she's pleased she hasn't told her face. She keeps dropping hints that I should go out and get a summer job. I tried telling her that I'm writing a novel and that I couldn't be expected to put that aside just to earn £3.37 an hour scanning carb-heavy food down at Aldi.

'Writing a novel?' she sniffed. 'Is that what you were doing when you came home last night at three in the morning singing a rude song?'

'That was research,' I explained. 'My novel features a binge-drinking teenager whose wild-haired mother doesn't understand her.'

As for my so-called friends — well, huh. They're nowhere to be seen most of the time. Here's a quick round-up:

As I mentioned, Al, my sort-of-boyfriend, has gone off

with his family on some kind of eco-holiday in South America. As I sit here looking out at the drizzle of an English summer, he's on the other side of the world counting turtles' eggs on a sun-kissed beach. Jugs, my on-again, off-again best friend has got herself a job working nights at the twenty-four-hour Tesco near Clifton. She sleeps all day so I never get to see her. I do ring her up from time to time to give her the skinny on *Come Dine With Me* while she's stacking shelves. Well it helps both of us pass the time.

Jake and Crumpet are all loved-up and totally unenthusiastic when I invited myself around for the evening last week, even though I brought the DVD box-set of *The Hills* series three. Happy couples are so dull. Will I go to hell for hoping they break up soon?

Poops is on holiday with his folks at their villa in Spain. I occasionally get texted blurry images of him dancing with extremely tanned girls not wearing very much. Good luck to him, I say. So glad he dumped that awful Lauren girl he was going out with a few weeks ago. Hi Lauren, if you're reading.

The Boy, my sort-of-ex, is working at the Asda distribution centre in Doncaster and has even got himself a little flat in the town. He pays next-to-nothing for it as the owner got caught in the credit crunch and is over the moon just to get any money at all. I got a text from him the other day asking me to go and stay with him because he felt lonely being just about the only person living in a new-build tower block. I politely refused. I'm not going there again, even if he does seem to have cleaned up his act. The Boy is not to be trusted, as I discovered when I lent him my bike after he drove his Renault Clio into Imogen Chivers's swimming pool. He came back the next week with a different bike.

'That's not my bike,' I told him.

He looked at it, puzzled. 'Well whose is it then?'

'I couldn't tell you that,' I said. 'All I know is that it's not mine.'

We both looked at it for a while. It was a nice bike, I'm not suggesting otherwise. Nicer than mine, in fact.

'Where did you get it?' I asked.

'Ah,' he said. 'Well, there's a story about that.'

'Go on.'

'I rode your bike to a gig,' he said. 'And I did what you said and put the lock-thing on.'

'So far so good,' I replied, encouragingly.

'But when I came out I was . . .'

'Drunk?' I suggested.

'Let's just say *disoriented*,' he responded. 'The code on your lock didn't seem to work so I had to break it.'

'Do you suppose the code on my lock wasn't working because it was actually someone else's lock?' I asked.

'That is possible,' he said, nodding.

Dear God in heaven . . .

My Allerton friends Emily and Trina are around most of the time, and I've been going out with them a bit, but they're both off to Europe next week with their families so I'll be on my tod again. Also had a bit of a falling-out with Trina, though I'm going to resist describing that on the blog as I'm hopeful we can patch things up. I've learned my lesson when it comes to blogging about the various social conflicts I get myself embroiled in, or at least not while they're still going on.

Anyway, this isn't getting us anywhere with the original point of this entry, which is to tell you all why I've decided to start writing the blog again. The thing is, I'd started thinking maybe Mum was right, maybe I should get a job. As it happens, I decided to pop into the *East Bucks Herald* offices and ask if they need a fashion reporter or social events columnist or something equally suited to the unique brand that is Miss Understanding.

I'm afraid it didn't go so well. I didn't have time to shave my legs so I wore tights and a knee-length pencil skirt, which were a little warm to be honest but I did look well businessy. I even put on some heels that Cheryl had passed down to me.

'Hello,' I said to the man at the desk, wobbling a little. 'I'm a writer and am looking for a summer job. Do you have any vacancies?' Then I smiled at him and tried to look open and interested like it had said to do in the handout the Guidance Counsellor gave me months ago. In hindsight I think I probably came over a bit deranged because he flinched a little and took a step backwards.

'Do you have any experience working in journalism?' he asked.

'I used to write an agony column on the school website, but they threw me off for er . . . excessive honesty,' I explained. 'Since then I've just been keeping a blog.'

'A blog,' he said flatly, as if he encountered wannabe journalists who write blogs *all the time*.

'It's a good blog,' I said. 'People actually read it. It's not just my mum.'

He laughed at that, thought for a bit, then said. 'How do you feel about working odd hours?'

'Don't mind at all,' I said, excited by the idea of working through the night to make a deadline. I've done it often enough writing History essays. Or at least cutting and pasting History essays off the internet.

'What about travel?' he said. 'The job I have in mind involves plenty of travel.'

'I LOVE travel,' I said, beaming. 'Would you pay expenses?'

'No,' he said. 'But I can lend you a bike if you don't have one.'

'A bike?' I asked, confused.

'Yes,' he said. 'How else would you deliver the papers?'

Hilarious. Why are older people all such smart-arses? Still, I suppose you have to start somewhere. I told him I'd think it over and get back to him.

Surely I can't be the only one having a rubbish time this summer? Please write in and let me know what a crap time you're having, so as to make me feel better. To keep things fresh I've decided to drop Blue-Sky Corner and do a new item – Top Five Feedback, where I list the best five comments on whatever topic we're on about. This week: The Top Five Things You Hate About Summer:

Laters alligators

Miss Understanding

Email from Anya to Jugs

Hi Babe

Hmph, had such a row with my 'new' friend Trina today. She read my blog and phoned me like five minutes later with her attitude on. Thing is she's quite good friends with Al and she rang up to yell at me for 'leading him on'. I'm totally not doing that at all. I really like him, and I told her that. 'So why won't you just commit to him?' she says and I went off on one. 'What do you want me to do? Tattoo his name on my arm? Beg him to impregnate me? Marry him?' I hate this part of a relationship, when you stop laughing and getting on, and you start having talks about 'the way things are going'.

Honestly, Jugs. What's wrong with just having an occasional date and a quick snog outside Holland and Barrett once a week? Why does everything need to get so heavy so quickly? Sigh, once he's back from South America I suppose we'll have 'a talk'.

How're you, anyway? Hope your Mum's OK.

Love

Anya

Miss Understanding Blog Entry
– 14th July, supplemental

Wow! Big news.

Jocasta has finally come up with the goods. It's only taken approximately sixteen years but everything's suddenly clicked and she's put in a strong bid for Parent of the Year Award. I think she's in with a real chance too, as long as the other finalists are Ozzy Osbourne and Jordan. I went down for dinner after telling her about my disappointment at the newspaper office.

'Yes, well, I've been talking to your father about that,' she said, stirring a pot of mung beans. 'Are you going to take the job?'

'Dunno. It means getting up at 5.00 am,' I said. 'I've never been awake that early before. I've heard bad things about 5.00 am.'

At this point I expected to get a lecture about responsibility, and learning the value of money, and the importance of building character and so on, but she surprised me, my mother. She put down her spoon and came over to face me.

'There is another option, you know?' she said.

'What's that?' I asked, expecting some kind of plumbing-based solution.

'Work experience,' she said.

'Do you get paid for that?' I asked hopefully.

Mum shook her head. 'No, but you'd get expenses. And if you really would like to do it, and do it properly, your father has agreed to pay you an allowance.' She raised her eyebrows waiting for my reaction.

'That sounds great,' I said, slightly stunned and highly suspicious. 'But why would he agree to pay me an allowance? He already gives me a bit every month.'

And then she hit me with the bombshell. 'He'd need to pay you a lot more if you were living in London. You'd need to buy food and Tube fares and what-not.'

'London?' I said, not quite getting it. I goggled at her for a bit. 'Why London?' I asked finally.

'Because that's where all the important publishers are,' she said, rolling her eyes at my ignorance. She turned back to stir the bubbling pot, hair floating in the breeze from the open window.

I sat and reflected on what she was saying. 'You mean I'd be doing work experience for a publisher in

London, getting money from Dad, living in London, on my own . . .'

'Not so fast, Peaches,' Mum said. 'We're not going to just let you loose in Sin City. Your father will be checking up on you REGULARLY. You'd be staying in his London flat in Docklands, of course. I asked him about this on the phone last night. As you know, he usually only stays there two or three nights a week.'

'Wow,' was all I could think of to say.

'Plus Marley and I'll come down and check on you from time to time,' she continued. I watched a blob of glutinous, yet wholesome, muck drop off the end of her spoon, onto her Birkenstocks. 'There will be no boys, no parties, no boys, no loud music and no boys.'

'You've already spoken to Dad about this?' I asked. 'You've arranged it all without telling me?'

Mum shrugged. 'I made enquiries, pulled a few strings. We were going to suggest it in a few days if you didn't come up with something yourself,' she said, scraping something congealed off the Aga lid and putting it back in the pot. 'I wasn't really sure you had the motivation but when you decided for yourself this morning to go off and find a job I decided you were old enough to do this, if it's what you want.' She peered over her shoulder at me, intently. 'Is it what you want?' she asked.

'Yes, of course it's what I want,' I said instantly. Up until three minutes ago I hadn't known this was what I wanted but now I felt I'd die if I wasn't allowed to go. Imagine being in London, working for a publisher, making contacts, learning the ins and outs of the world of book publishing. This could be a step towards becoming a published author!

'But where could I work?' I said, realizing that specific and kind of important issue hadn't yet been broached.

'I've already got that sorted,' Mum said casually, though I could see a self-satisfied smile twitching at the corner, of her mouth. She pulled some bowls out of a cupboard and began spooning slop into them. 'You know Seth's mother, don't you?'

Lance chose that moment to walk into the kitchen, unbeknown to Mum, who had her back to him. He took one look at the slop-doling operation, looked at me, raised a finger to his lips and slipped a curry menu out from under a magnet on the fridge before disappearing as silently as he'd come.

'Yes of course . . . Portia something.'

'Portia Bolt-Hodges. She's one of my oldest friends, so for God's sake don't go running off at the mouth and offending her, OK?'

I gave her a hurt look. What could she mean?

'She also happens to own Boxwood Press,' Mum went on. 'In the West End. I've spoken to her. She'd be happy to have you work there for a couple of months.'

'Really?' I said. 'How hard did you pull these strings, Mum?'

'Hard enough. You can start on Monday.'

And she leaned back against the Aga, a smug look on her face. I stood up, gave her a hug and did a little dance. Marley came in to see what the fuss was about and decided to join in the fun by bouncing up and down. Then he slipped over on some spilled casserole and pulled the spice rack off the wall as he went down.

We all fell about laughing. Happy families again. She's not that bad I suppose, my mum.

And so that's that. As of Monday I will no longer be Miss Understanding, unemployed, sullen teen of Allerton, Bucks, I will be Miss Understanding, glamorous editorial assistant of Boxwood Press, London.

More soon

Miss Understanding

Miss Understanding Blog Entry
– 18th July 2010, Docklands

Howdy Sports Fans

Don't think I haven't noticed that since I have stopped the agony column my blog readership has dropped to about three people (and I know Joca65 is you, Mother), but I'm going to keep on blogging anyway because I'm more vain than a giraffe's jugular. Besides, I'm a writer at heart and everything that comes out of a writer's head needs to be saved and backed up in case you find a use for it later. When one is a writer one thinks even a shopping list is worth backing up. Nonetheless, I did get a few responses to my request . . . no, my *demand* for suggestions on what you hate about summer. Here are the best:

Hellgirl wrote in to say she hates summer because you're forced to expose bits of your body even *you* don't want to see, let alone show to anyone else. I'm with you there girl, and if you're talking about the bits I think you're talking about, I got mine sunburned last year. Both of them.

Ben Noakes hates that 'vague guilty feeling you get for not making the most of the sunshine when all you want to do is sit inside and play Tetris 3D'. I know what you mean, Ben. My mum's boyfriend Lance gets around the problem by sitting outside with a can of lager whilst watching Wimbledon through the sitting-room window.

'Worst thing about summer?' writes Grimble. 'Family days out when no one in the family wants to go.' I feel for you, Grimble. I blame the weekend newspapers for producing those Top Five Things to Do with the Kids this Summer, everyone assumes everyone else really wants to go to Banbury World of String (free parking) and they're just putting up with it for the greater good.

Charlie Chambers can't stand it when his friends come back from fantastic Caribbean holidays browner than a chocolate-coated Peter Andre while he's still sneezing from the cold he picked up in Weston-super-Mare.

I was delighted to hear from our old friend Gex, who reserves his bile for festivals. 'THEY IS SHIT BRUV,' he informs me, via text. 'YOU EITHER GO AND HAVE A SHIT TIME IN A PILE OF MUD, OR YOU DON'T GO AND HAVE 2 LISTEN TO YOUR M8S GOING ON ABOUT HOW WICKED THE TUNES WERE AND HOW THEY ALL GOT OFF WITH LOADS OF HOS AND THEN TELLING YOU HOW YOU MISSED OUT INNIT.'

So I think we're all agreed there. Summer sucks the left one.

Now, for those of you who *are* interested, I'm here! In London. At Dad's flat in Docklands. I've been here before of course, but never stayed over so I've never been here at night. The view is amazing. I can see little orange and white lights stretching out to the horizon. I can see little planes taking off from City airport a few miles away. I can see the Dome lit up like an electrified Christmas cake. I can even see the Thames from the balcony, winding through the city like a fat, black snake. It's all so beautiful.

Dad helped me move in, and introduced me to the security guard. His name's Raj. He's really nice, has enormous sideburns and thick glasses, a sort of Asian version of Jemaine from Flight of the Conchords. 'Hello Miss Buxton,' he said. 'You just missed my friend Geoff, he's a male stripper at a club in the City.'

'Really?' I asked as my dad tutted loudly behind me.

'Oh yes, but he's knocking on a bit now,' Raj said, straight-faced. 'He was thinking of retiring recently but he's decided to stick it out for another year.'

'Very good,' I said.

'Thanks Raj,' said Dad. 'If you must tell jokes to my daughter, please keep them clean, would you?'

Raj winked at me as Dad led me into the lift.

Mum and Marley are here too, by the way. Dad left as

Mum arrived and now we've ordered a pizza. We persuaded Mum to let us get two, one with meat on account of the fact that we weren't under her roof any more so were in carnivore mode. Marley's trying to work out how to unlock the parental control on the Sky Box and Mum's trying to work out how to unlock the drinks cabinet. They're going to stay for a few days until I get settled. I'm glad because it's all a little unnerving, really. I can't wait to start work tomorrow.

Pizza's here. More later.

Anya

Miss Understanding Blog Entry
– 19th July 2010

Sorry. Didn't have a chance to write any more last night. Things got a bit out of hand. Marley ate too much pizza, bounced up and down on the sofa and was promptly sick all over it. I found myself surfing the net looking for tips on how to get tomato sauce and mozzarella-flavoured vomit out of suede. In case you're interested, the best way turns out to be putting a cushion on top of the stain and leaving it there for ever.

Anyway, here I am at Boxwood Press, finally. I'm writing this on the work computer, which I'm probably not supposed to be doing, but no one told me I couldn't. Do whatever you want until someone asks you to stop. That's my new motto. Not sure who I heard it from but it sounds like good advice to me. But come to think of it, no one's told me hardly anything at all. Portia had me sitting in Reception for nearly half an hour this morning. Her secretary said she was in a meeting and would be down in a moment. I sat and watched the lifts for a bit, so imagine my surprise at seeing her arrive through the front doors twenty-five minutes later having obviously just arrived from home. And she looked straight through me! I had to wave my hand in front of her face before she even recognized me. I should have known, I suppose. After all, this is one of my mother's oldest friends we're talking about – we've only known each other since, hmm, well, since I was born, come to think of it.

Let me tell you about the job. I love it so far. Though I have no idea what I'm doing yet. My 'mentor' is Claire Simmonds. Portia basically bundled me through the door to her office and said, 'Claire dear, this is Anya. I have to dash.' Portia then disappeared into her office where she spent the rest of the day with the blinds closed.

'Are you the new girl from Contracts?' Claire asked, looking confused.

'Er no,' I said, hoping there hadn't been a terrible mix-up and that I wasn't supposed to be working in Contracts. 'I'm the new work experience girl, in Editorial?'

It turns out she was expecting me next week, hence the confusion. Phew. Claire seems nice, but a little tired-looking. She looks like she should be pretty but has slightly mousy hair which could do with some serious root lift. 'I'm a commissioning editor,' she explained. 'Do you understand how things work at a publisher's?'

'A little, I suppose,' I said, feeling nervous. 'The editors decide if books are worth publishing or not?'

She shrugged. 'Sort of. The Sales department decide that ultimately. If we can't make money from a book we don't publish it.'

'Even if it's brilliant?' I asked.

She sighed. 'If it's really brilliant we might publish it. But we do have a lot of brilliant books sitting in the warehouse going slowly yellow.'

She showed me around the office, introduced me to a few people and got me settled at a desk. My OWN desk. I even have a computer.

They've given me a big pile of manuscripts to read (the slush pile). These are what they call 'unsolicited manuscripts' and apparently Boxwood is one of the few remaining publishers to accept them. Basically, randoms send in their masterpieces, hoping that an editor will think their story is brilliant, send round a truck full of cash and make them into the new Stephenie Meyer. Needless to say, and no offence to any of you out there who have done this, they're mostly rubbish. I mean, you'd think people would use a spell checker before they print off, right? God bless them, though, you've got to credit them with imagination.

Or mental illness. Take the one I looked at today: *Francisco Drake and the Mystical Nachos:*

There's this duck called Francisco and it eats a nacho that has accidentally fallen into the lake and it loves it so much it decides to swim to Mexico to find where all the nachos come from and has loads of adventures on the way and that.

There was what looked like a child's drawing of an armadillo stuck to the back, not sure what that was all about. Anyway, my job is to reply with the standard thanks-but-no-thanks letter:

> Dear Blank
> Thank you for your submission _____ which we read with interest. Whilst the setting was vivid and some of the characterisation very strong, we didn't love it enough to really feel we could champion it properly. We wish you luck with your writing career.
> Yours sincerely
> Anya Buxton
> Assistant to Claire Simmonds

If any of them are any good, I am to pass them to Posh Katie, the editorial assistant. She mostly snorts and rejects them immediately. 'Too derivative!' she says, handing them back. Derivative of what, though? Derivative of something rubbish I suppose.

Anyway, better go as it's the tea round now. Portia insists on her Earl Grey infusing for five minutes, it's quite a responsibility . . .

Love

Miss Understanding

Miss Understanding Blog Entry
– 20th July 2010

Thanks for your emails. In answer to some questions I got:

Fat Gareth – no you cannot come and stay with me. I don't mean to be rude, but . . . NO.

Jenna Hall – yes, of course you are free to send in a manuscript for our consideration, but no, we do not publish erotic fiction here at Boxwood. Even if it *is* very tasteful.

Willow Thomas – yes, I promise that if the girl from Contracts doesn't show up, I'll let you know and your unemployed older sister Blossom can apply for the job. No I don't know what people in Contracts do either.

Remember yesterday I told you I have a new motto? Do whatever you want until someone tells you to stop? Well, it got me wondering if you lot have any good proverbs or mottos you try to live by – write in and tell me and I'll post the best five. It'll give me something to do, because I must say, Blogpals, I'm feeling a teensy bit bored. No one's giving me anything to do. Apart from the slush pile and the tea-making, my only other duties are opening Claire's post, which is mostly invitations to dull-sounding literary events or unsolicited manuscripts which go straight onto the slush pile anyway. And while I'm having a moan, no one's talking to me. I said good morning to some bloke in the kitchen and he just grunted. It's like everyone thinks just because I'm here only temporarily that they don't have to treat me like a real person. This must be what it's like to be last year's *Big Brother* winner.

The only people I do have human contact with are Katie, who sits opposite me, so she doesn't really have much choice, and Claire, who occasionally wafts past in a cloud of Nivea deodorant, lost in her own world.

I've just sent her an email.

Email from Anya to Claire

Hi Claire

Thanks for letting me look through the slush pile. It has been instructive and at times highly entertaining but doesn't entirely fill my day. Are there any other duties you could let me have while I'm here? I'm so keen to learn as much as I can about publishing during my period of work experience.

Yours

Anya

Wow!

Three minutes after I sent that email she came out of her office and stood over me. Uh-oh, I thought, what have I done?

'Anya,' she said. 'there's no need to send me formal emails. If you want more work just pop your head around my door, OK?'

I nodded, feeling embarrassed. I could sense Katie smirking across from me.

'Here,' said Claire, dumping a big pile of typewritten paper on my desk. 'Read through this and tell me if you spot any typos or grammatical mistakes. Sorry about the jam on that one, that was from my breakfast.' Then she walked off. I flicked my gaze up to Katie, who was looking a bit sniffy.

'Pssst,' I hissed at Katie. 'A typo's a spelling mistake, right?'

She looked a little smug and nodded in a superior fashion. 'It's short for typographical error,' she informed me. 'Anything else you want to know, Anya, just ask.'

Well look at me, Blogpals. I'm an editor.

Miss Understanding

Email from Anya to Jugs

Hi Jugs

HELLO? I realize you're in training for the London 2012

31

sleeping-all-bloody-day event but it would be nice if you roused yourself from hibernation once in a while to send me an email.

Anyway, I just wanted to fill you in on the inside story on the job. There's only so much I can say on the blog. Not that I think anyone at work's reading it, they have better things to do than scan the ramblings of a sixteen-year-old. It's just that after the assorted confusions, cock-ups and embarrassments I caused earlier in the year with the whole agony thing, I think I need to be a little more careful what I make public. For example, I decided not to say anything at all about Jenna Hall having her stomach pumped twice in one week. Or about Fat Gareth and Kayleigh Leach finally getting off with each other in the ladies' loos at Milton Keynes' indoor skiing centre. I'm reformed. Like Take That.

Anyway, first let me tell you about Katie, the girl I sit opposite at Boxwood. She's otherwise known as Snooty McSnobface. She's sooo irritating. For a start she sniffs the whole time. Every thirty seconds or so I just hear this little *sniff* and it's doing my head in. She doesn't talk to me much except to bitch about other staff members, none of whom I know. I don't really feel I can tell her to shut up, but neither can I go along with her little bile-fests. I just sit there, shrug and pull that 'oh dear' face.

She's particularly mean about Portia. Katie reckons she never does any work, just sits in her office all day and phones her friends.

'Every so often,' Katie says, 'she lets rip the most enormous fart. I suppose she thinks we can't hear with the door closed.' Then she laughs like a drain.

TMI, Katie.

'She has the most gorgeous son though,' she told me. 'His name's Seth and he's totally dreamy. Completely loaded too. Ideal husband material. I keep hoping she'll bring him along to an office party, but no luck so far.'

I haven't told her that Jocasta is one of those friends Portia spends all day on the phone to, nor that I know Seth and have his phone number. I'm looking forward to seeing her face when she finds out though. So what if Portia never does any work? It's her company, she can do what she likes, right?

She's an odd one, Katie. On the surface she's uber-posh, but underneath the Joanna Lumley voice you can just about detect this slight Norfolk accent if you listen carefully. I swear I heard her say 'compooh-urr' the other day. She has some strange pronunciations. Today she asked me to go and see Sandra, the lady who guards the stationery cupboard, to get her a memo pad, only Katie pronounced it 'meemo'. I was sure that wasn't right, but who was I to say? I duly asked Sandra for a 'meemo' pad

33

and she laughed. 'It's pronounced memmo,' she said, like she was talking to a retard.

I KNOW that! Now Sandra thinks I'm an idiot.

The other thing I really don't like about Katie is she's one of those girls who always looks you up and down, checking out what you're wearing.

Then she sniffs.

Other people I've met are:

Giuseppe: The post-room boy. Who is not a boy at all, but a middle-aged Italian bloke who barks at people in the corridors. At first I thought he was a kindred spirit as most people don't talk to him either, unless they're asking him where the hell their very urgent parcel might have got to. But I went off him when Katie pointed out that he keeps popping his head over my partition and having a good old look down my top.

Claire: My boss, who is actually nice if a little moody. And the cat thing weirds me out a bit. She's constantly covered in cat hair and, according to Katie, her house is over-run with them. She also leaves bits of food over all the manuscripts. Sometimes we get queries from authors asking whether the mark on page thirty-eight is a new typographical symbol or just a dried tomato seed.

Mad Jack: The foul-tempered production manager who grunts at me in the kitchen in the morning. He and I both like strong coffee, so we sometimes nod at each

34

other as one coffee afficionado to another. Yesterday he even spoke to me. 'Are you the new girl from Contracts?' he said.

'No,' I replied, 'I'm here on work experience, in Editorial.'

'Oh,' he said, and we left it there. I pity the new girl in Contracts. When she finally gets here she's got a lot to live up to.

And that's it really. I just sit at my desk, listening to Katie sniff, reading manuscripts and doing the tea round every hour. Not sure what I was expecting, but some sort of human contact would be nice. I keep wondering if I should ask Katie if she wants to go for a sandwich but I'm scared she'll just sniff and totally reject me. I'm also scared that she'll say yes and assume that means we're friends. If that happens then I'm convinced she'll start droning on about fashion labels I've never heard of and making me swap iPods so I can listen to bands I don't like.

God, I miss you guys. I miss Al too (though that's another thing I wouldn't put on my blog.) How's life at Tesco's?

Love

Anya

Miss Understanding Blog Entry
– 21st July 2010

Thanks for all your proverbs, I have to say some of them seemed slightly far-fetched. Just look at the first one.

1) 'Early to bed and early to rise, makes Fat Gareth healthy, wealthy and wise.' I mean honestly. More like 'Early to bed, late to rise and in between stuff face full of pies'.

2) Saskia Garfield is a bit more thoughtful. 'Whatever your mum tells you, do the opposite,' is her guide to life. Fair enough Saskia, if your mum's anything like mine, half the time she tells you things she's just made up on the spot, and the other half she deliberately tells you the opposite of the truth to try and put you off. So following your advice means you'll be right seventy-five percent of the time.

3) 'Build a man a fire, and he'll be warm for a day,' says Guy DuLancey, presumably having been reading his *SAS*

Survival Handbook again. 'But set a man on fire, and he'll be warm for the rest of his life,' he chortles. Sigh . . .

4) Tooz writes in with this mysterious saying: 'If someone offers me something, I always say yes straight away.' So far so good. 'If I then decide I don't want it, I just leave it on the side of the plate.' That's brilliant Tooz, thanks for that. Only thing is, what if it's not food that the person's offering? What happens, Tooz, if you don't have a plate to leave it on?

5) My favourite though is from Jez Morton, who writes to say, 'I always assume everyone I meet is a good bloke and I try to see the best in people. Mostly I'm not disappointed.' That's really heart-warming Jez, though you need to watch out you don't take this whole 'everyone's lovely' thing too far, that's the mistake Sharon Osbourne made too often on *X Factor*. Sometimes you need to identify the timewasters nice and early.

I took the manuscript home with me last night so I could hand it back to Claire first thing this morning. Thing was I couldn't concentrate with Mum and Marley charging about the place slamming doors and fighting over the remote.

'When are you going home?' I asked.

Mum looked at me in surprise. 'I thought we'd agreed we'd stay until you were settled?'

'I am settled,' I replied. 'Or at least I would be settled if Marley didn't keep barging into the bathroom as soon as I step into the shower.'

'In his defence,' Mum said, 'there are no locks on any of the doors in the flat. This is such a man's flat. Men don't bother with closing doors when they're in the bathroom.'

'Or the toilet,' I said, eying Marley coldly. He was lying on the back bit of the sofa listening to my iPod and eating a cheese string.

'Anya,' Mum said. 'We'll stay until I'm comfortable with leaving you on your own, OK?'

I was ready to argue, but figured I'd just shoot myself in the foot if we had a row. With that twisted logic mothers have, there's no way she'd leave if she was mad at me. So I tried a different tactic. I went into my room (Did I mention it has a view of Canary Wharf? Totally awesome but that flashing light on the top can get a little annoying in the middle of the night if you haven't closed the blinds properly) and made a phone call.

'Hello?'

'Hi Lance, it's Anya.'

'Hello Anya,' he said. 'I thought you'd gone to live in London.'

'I have. Problem is, so have Mum and Marley.'

'Oh I see,' he said getting it instantly. 'And you want to get rid of them so you can have the flat to yourself for parties and all the rest of it.'

'Well, now you come to mention it, yes I suppose I do. But more immediately I want to be able to walk around the flat without standing on a piece of jammy toast or an empty wine bottle.'

'Ah,' he said. 'Speaking for myself, I was rather enjoying the peace and quiet round here.'

Not for the first time, I found myself wondering whether Lance had actually moved in with Mum. With us. He seemed to be around pretty much every night. I decided it was a question for another time.

'And being able to get into the bathroom in the morning would be a help,' I continued. 'I haven't had time to pluck my eyebrows since we've been here and they're well overdue. I look like a character from *Sesame Street*.'

'OK, I understand,' he said. 'But what can I do about it?'

'Can't you engineer some kind of emergency back in Allerton?' I suggested. 'Nothing too serious, but enough to make her come back home.'

'Hmmm,' he said, dubiously.

'She just wants to feel needed, Lance,' I said, fearing I was losing him. 'You do need her, don't you?'

There was a rather longer pause than I'd anticipated. 'Yes,' he said finally.

I breathed a sigh of relief.

'OK,' he said. 'I'll think of something.'

Email from Jugs to Anya – Friday 23rd July 2010

Hey Bird

Nice to hear from you, I thought you would have forgotten about us poor mountain folk now you're in the fleshpots. Have you been to Soho yet? If the whole publishing thing doesn't work out I hear there's good money to be made there for adventurous girls. I've been reading the blog – if you're trying to disguise the fact you don't think much of Katie it's not really working, OK?

Tesco is all right, though my boss is a cow. She's totally corporate and one of those people who think they're so important they have to use acronyms and abbreviations all the time so as not to waste time saying proper words. It's all 'ETA this' and 'POD that' and 'We have to unload this container PDQ or else we'll have a V big problem'. I feel like telling her to F Off.

I'm squirrelling all the money away for college, so am quite glad I'm working nights, it reduces the temptation to blow it all on Tia Maria-and-Coke down at The Bell. Also everyone's scattered to the four winds so there's no one to party with anyway. You're in London, Crumpet and Jake are holed up in Love Cottage, The Boy's now an

upstanding citizen of Doncaster. Poops is working his
way through the STD capital of Iberia.

So all's well but a bit dull. Let me know if you're
coming back to Allerton anytime soon, I'll try and
visit, OK?

Love

Jugs

Miss Understanding Blog Entry
– 26th July 2010

Sorry, I haven't had time to read through everyone's emails. I'm too busy exploring my new surroundings here in Docklands. There's a fitness centre in the building which I'm allowed to use, that's so cool! I feel like a pop star popping down to my exclusive gym (I'm the only person who ever seems to use it; most of the residents here are a little crusty, shall we say). The pop star feeling wears off a bit when I get back to the flat and find Marley running around with no pants on, but that just helps me to keep it real I suppose.

Let me tell you about my journey to work and back every day. I take the Underground from Canary Wharf. That's the station they always use in *Spooks* and in zombie films, you can hardly move for film crews most mornings. It's the Jubilee line (the grey one) and I get off at Bond St, which is the closest station to Cavendish

Square, where Boxwood's offices are. I come up out of the Tube on Oxford St and it's a four-minute walk from there.

It doesn't take long before you become a proper Londoner, you know? Day One you're standing on the wrong side of the escalator and smiling at people. By Day Five you're tutting at people who try to get on the train without letting passengers off first.

Yesterday I found myself nipping in front of a lady with a pram to make sure I got my usual spot near the second door in the third carriage because that opens up right in front of the exit at Bond St and if I'm quick I can get ahead of everybody else by going down the tunnel that says No Entry and up the escalators etc.

By the end of the first week, you can tell when a train is coming by the feel of the wind on your face as you walk down the access tunnels. The harder the wind, the closer the train and the more you have to hurry to catch it. Oh, and you soon learn not to smile at people. Especially if they are an old man with an imaginary Bluetooth and a carrier bag full of Tennents Extra.

I do quite like the journey though, I feel alive on the Tube and I love watching (surreptitiously) all the people getting on and off. I wonder what their lives are like, where they live, where they're going. You can spot straight away the people who do the journey every day, they look controlled and a little vacant. Then there are the tourists stumbling about and thumping people with their ginormous backpacks. They always look at the map in total mystification for a minute or so, then point at it, turn to their companions and say, '*Okford Sorkos*'. The third group are loonies and beggars, who can be a little scary but you just have to ignore them. Finally there are People from the North who try to talk to strangers knowing full well they're going to be disappointed. They only do it so they can go back to the North and say, 'Eee it's good to be back. Bloody Londoners are so rude, won't even look at you on the Underground' etc.

The office is in a modern construction amongst a load of Georgian buildings and despite being three hundred years younger it's looking a little tired. In fact it's looking not just *tired* but positively *off-colour* and perhaps even a little *pre-menstrual*. Katie told me Boxwood had moved in twenty years ago. I suppose the office must have been cutting-edge décor then, glass and steel everywhere, midnight-blue carpets, pastel vertical blinds, open-brick walls. Boxwood was the first London publisher to give computers to all the staff.

Now the décor looks a bit shabby, many of the vertical blinds are lying horizontally amongst the mouse crap on the faded carpet, and I reckon my computer is one of the original ones handed out – it's practically steam-driven. I'm wondering about asking if I can use my laptop instead.

Well, that's all for now, I'm zonked. More tomorrow, unless I get invited to go to after-work drinks, which is not likely. Today Katie went out with some of the Publicity girls. The Publicity department organizes events to promote books and authors. They're always off to this glamorous literary festival or that swanky lunch. She didn't invite me. They seem quite nice but a bit snooty and she hasn't introduced me to them so I could hardly just invite myself could I?

Much love

Anya

Miss Understanding Blog Entry
– 27th July 2010

This morning Claire swung by my desk to see how I was getting on. I handed back the manuscript she'd asked me to proofread the other day.

'It's fantastic!' I said.

'Really?' she replied, raising an eyebrow.

'Um, well, not fantastic,' I said. 'I wasn't sure if you wanted me to be enthusiastic or . . .'

'Honest?' she prompted.

'Yes, honest.'

'Always be honest, Anya,' she said.

'OK,' I replied, nodding.

'Honesty might not get you very far in life,' she went on, 'but you'll feel better about where you end up.'

'Erm OK,' I said. 'Thanks. In that case, I didn't think it was very good at all. I'm not really into fairies, or unicorns. So book five in a series about fairies riding winged unicorns didn't exactly keep me gripped to the last page.'

'If you were the Finance Director you'd be enthralled by the sales figures,' she said.

'Each to their own, I suppose,' I shrugged. 'I marked up a few typos and suggested a couple of things that could be rewritten to make them clearer.'

'Thanks,' she said, flicking through the pages. Then she looked down at me. 'Would you like to do more of these?'

'Yes,' I said. 'I'd love to do more, y'know, meaty work.'

'I'll see what I can find for you,' she said.

When I got home I found Mum packing.

'Where are all your clothes?' she shouted at Marley, who was standing on the balcony in his underpants and spitting over the side.

'I dunno,' he said.

'I packed three pairs of trousers, four shirts, five pairs of socks and about a hundred pairs of underpants for you before we came,' she said, rummaging through a concealed wardrobe in Dad's room where she'd been sleeping. 'Now I can only find one pair of trousers, two shirts and three single socks, none of which match,' she said, worriedly. 'And I can't find any underpants at all. I just can't understand it.'

'You're going then?' I asked hopefully.

'Yes,' Mum said absently. 'Lance phoned to say the timer on the video machine's not working properly and it doesn't seem to be taping *New Tricks*.'

'Mum that's awful,' I said. 'You miss one of those and that's it, you'll never catch up.'

'I know,' she said grimly.

Marley stomped in, looking grumpy. 'When are we going?' he asked.

'Quarter of an hour,' Mum replied quickly.

'That's *ages*!' he whined.

'OK, we'll go in fifteen minutes,' she said.

'Cool,' he nodded and went off again.

'So I thought you seemed fine here at the weekend . . .' Mum went on. 'And your father will be here tonight and . . . ah!' She held up a sock, grinning in triumph. 'Found one!'

'Brilliant,' I said.

Email to Anya from Al

Hey you

Just a quick message. Dad brought me, my sisters and Marina into town to pick up some supplies for the camp and he's given us fifteen minutes to pop into the only internet café for a thousand miles. We're all really keen to get back because the turtles have started to hatch. Yesterday we saw three different caches open up and these tiny little turtles come flapping and scrabbling out of the white sand. It was amazing, I really wish you could have been here.

Marina and I got as close as we were allowed and watched them look about, then head straight towards the sea. We knew this bit was going to be tough to watch but it was also quite uplifting. The thing is, most of the turtles get snatched up and eaten by seabirds before they get to the water. It's natural selection in action. Time after time we'd see these brave little fellows popping their heads out and waddling determinedly down towards the sea only to watch them being grabbed by some great squawking monster. I don't mind admitting I filled up a bit. Poor Marina was bawling and I had to give her a hug. But it was so brilliant when they made it, and dozens of them did. I tried to think about the exciting, long lives they were going to lead out there in the deep blue ocean.

We've been spending virtually all our time on the beach. We swim a bit but you have to watch out for sharks, they say. Next week we're going on a trek up to a big waterfall in the forest. Should be fantastic.

Oops, Dad's here, gotta go. Miss you heaps, write soon, I hope to be back in a town next week.

Love

Al

Miss Understanding Blog Entry
– 28th July 2010

Oh my God, bloody big news!

I've been given an author to look after! I'm really excited. Claire broke the news in her office. It was the first time I'd actually been properly inside it. I'd only ever just stuck my head through the door previously.

It was difficult to concentrate on what she was saying at first, on account of all the photographs on her notice board. Creepy photos. Of her mean-looking cats. Plus I was sitting on a lever-arch file, due to a shortage of chairs and space. It's not comfortable, my bum is still numb from the experience.

'Right,' Claire said, 'Casper Williams.'

I gave her my blank look. If my face were a web browser it would have said: *Page not found*.

'Casper Williams? Our teenage best-selling author?'

'Oh, that Casper Williams,' I said, still none the wiser.

Claire peered at me over her glasses. 'Ask me no questions.'

'OK.'

'No, that's the name of his book,' Claire said slowly. '*Ask Me No Questions*.'

'Ooh yes,' I said, a vague memory of a poster in Reception drifted into my head. 'I've heard of that.'

'Excellent,' she went on, patiently. 'Have you read it?'

'No, autobiographies aren't my thing,' I said. I didn't tell her I'm too busy writing about my own life to read about someone else's.

'It's a science fiction novel,' she said, eyes narrowing as though she might be regretting asking me to do this. 'It won the Mulligan First-Time Writer Award.' She plucked a copy from the shelf above her desk and handed it over. 'It's good.'

'Great,' I said. Then she handed me a file.

'This is the correspondence we've had with Casper since the publication of *Ask Me No Questions*. With certain, er, commercially-sensitive letters removed. Read through it. Basically the deal is this,' she went on. 'He's contracted to write another book for us. *Ask Me No Questions* did so well for us that we're desperate for him to write another, but he's just not delivering. We don't know why. Contracts think he's trying to get out of his obligations so he can write for another publisher. I suspect he has writer's block and has just dried up but doesn't want to say. Portia thinks . . . well, she has another theory . . .'

I waited for her to elaborate, but she had already moved on.

'Anyway,' she said, shaking her head as if to clear it. 'He's sending us absolute rubbish. It's so bad that I can scarcely believe that it comes from the same Casper Williams – the infamous teenage prodigy – the genius who wrote our biggest-selling novel!' Her shoulders drooped. Thing is, we can't afford to lose him, he's our only big name. Plus we've already paid him for writing it. Unfortunately none of us has been able to get anywhere with him.'

I nodded, waiting for her to explain what all this had to do with me.

'So I want *you* to write to him,' she said finally, watching me closely.

'Me? But I'm not an editor, I wouldn't know what to say.'

'Portia tells me you fancy yourself as a bit of a wordsmith,' she said. 'And you're about the same age as him. We published *Questions* when he was fifteen, he's only eighteen now. I'm sure you have some weird street language you can use to bond with him.'

'Bitchin',' I said, trying to be funny.

Claire blinked. 'Whatever. The fact is that at this stage, I'll try anything, so please do what you can, won't you? Our profits are down this year and . . . quite frankly Anya, we need this.'

'Right. No pressure, then,' I said weakly, rising from the lever-arch file and hobbling to the door. 'I'll see what I can do.'

Upshot is I'm taking Casper's book home with me tonight. I'll start it on the Tube. I'll probably finish it too, if my journey into work is anything to go by.

Ciao for now.

Anya

Email from Anya to Al

Hi Al

Thanks for your email. It all sounds amazing. I'm totally jealous. BTW, who is Marina? Some local girl perhaps? Dusky-skinned with a 32D cup? More details on her please. And you don't say what you've been getting up to in the evenings with no telly. Some gaps need filling here.

Small point to make on the turtle situation. Why do you spend hours counting all the eggs only to sit on your arses and watch ninety percent of these endangered creatures get eaten by seagulls immediately after they've hatched?

Not telling you how you should be spending your time

or anything, but a small amount of flapping your arms about to frighten off the birds might give the little chaps a fighting chance of survival. Or, if that's too much effort, what about a scarecrow? Just a thought.

Maybe I'm not the best person to comment on conservation matters considering it was me who stepped on that rare frog and killed it when the zoo man came to give a talk at school last year. As I said at the time, if it was so damn precious, what was he doing carrying it in a box with enormous great holes in the side? And what did he expect to happen after a frog escapes into a room full of excitable teenage girls? I fully admit I got caught up in the mass hysteria and ran about flapping my arms. Under those circumstances I could hardly be expected to notice a small purple frog hopping into my path.

Anyway, be careful of man-eaters, both in and out of the water.

An

x

Email from Claire to Anya

Hi Anya

Here is some of the more recent correspondence I've had with Casper. I've forwarded it on to you in an attachment, but please don't send this on to anyone else, it's all confidential of course. Read through it and you'll get an idea of how . . . er . . . difficult he can be.

  Best

  Claire

Email from Casper to Claire

21st June 2010

Dear Ms Simmonds

Thank you for your email dated 12th June 2010 in response to my email of the 1st June 2010, which in turn was a response to your earlier email (in the same vein) dated 22nd May 2010 and so on right back to the very first email you sent me on this subject way back in August 2008. We were both much younger then.

I was a bit surprised by the tone of your letter, which at times comes across as a little hysterical. I appreciate that I am a bit late delivering the manuscript of the second book. But this isn't entirely my fault, as you know. Apart from the ongoing difficulties I have had with Davina, my cat, the lateness can in some part be said to be down to you rejecting every single idea and synopsis I have sent. It takes two to tango, as they say! How can I write the book if you've rejected it before I start?

Whilst in hindsight I realize that such ideas as *Natalie Cooper – Teen Nazi Hunter* and *Class 4b in Purgatory* might not have been suitable subjects for a children's book, I still don't see why you had to reject *Aslef – the Finless*

Sturgeon which approaches the issues of disability, environmentalism AND the Middle East crisis. (BTW, many thanks for pointing out that Aslef is not, as I thought, a popular boys' name on the Arabian peninsular and is in fact the name of a train drivers' union! Such fact-checking ability is why you've risen to the very tip-top of your noble profession.)

That said, you also rejected *Stephen and the Magic iPod*, which could very well have been the next Harry Potter had it been handled intelligently by a competent editor. J.K. was rejected dozens of times you know? Far be it for me to suggest similar levels of short-sightedness amongst today's editors.

I must say I was a little disheartened after reading your letter, but I soon 'regrouped' and shrugged off your latest efforts to stifle my creativity. As you know, I am nothing if not resilient, so to show there are no hard feelings, and that I am very keen to fulfil my contractual obligations, I enclose a synopsis for my latest idea for a series of children's books – *Tree Hostipal!* Kids love trees! And try as I might, I can find no similar books currently on the shelves.

You told me the market was 'saturated' with books about horses when I tried to pitch *Sherlock Hooves – Horse Detective* to you last year. Well, no such saturation with trees!

I look forward to the refresher cheque. Shall we say £5,000?

Yours sincerely

Casper Williams

PS Visited the vet's with Davina again this morning. Such a long wait. Heaven knows how long the bloke in front had been there, suffice to say he was after some ointment for his pterodactyl's beak infection. No wonder I never get any work done!

Attachment:

TREE HOSTIPAL!
Hook line: 'Leave' it to the professionals!

Gaby and Si's parents run a successful tree surgery in Newport. The kids just love trees and spend their whole time hanging around the operating theatre trying to help out with branch straightening and leaf shining, etc.

The first book: Storm in a Tree Cup *introduces the children and their faithful marmoset, Woodrot. During the Great Storms of 2007, their parents are called out to attend tree emergencies such as trees falling over and things getting blown into trees and damaging them. One stormy night, unnoticed by their parents, the kids go along for the ride and soon get into hot water.*

Woodrot saves the day, and when the children prove instrumental in saving a cute young beech sapling, their parents realize there's more to these kids than meets the eye!

Book Two: Axe Me No Questions *explores issues surrounding death and euthanasia. Gaby and Si's father occasionally goes out late at night carrying an axe. He comes home tired and harrowed, sometimes covered with sap. One stormy night, they follow him and discover the dark side of tree surgery.*

But when their closest tree friend, Old oaky Oaklestaff, gets a touch of Dutch Elm disease. It becomes a race against time to save him from Dad's sharp blade. Woodrot saves the day again, somehow.

Book Three: Barking up the Wrong Tree. *I'm still working on the plot line for this one but thought the title was so good it was worth including as is. Needless to say, Woodrot saves everyone's bacon.*

Here are some illustrations to help you visualize. I'm thinking Vernon Kay and Tess Daly as the parents in the inevitable film. As for the kids, one of the Olivers for Si, and that little girl off the cake ad for Gaby. The one with the walnuts.

Email from Claire to Casper

Dear Casper

Thank you for your email and submission Tree Hostipal (sic) dated 21st June. I have passed it on to my colleague Anya who will be editing you from now on. This is due to a reshuffle within the company. You will be hearing from her in the next few days.

Yours sincerely

Claire Simmonds

Senior Commissioning Editor

Email from Casper to Claire

Dear Claire

I'm sorry to hear you have been reshuffled. You shouldn't take this as a demotion, but as a move sideways. A chance to shine in areas more suited to your abilities.

Best wishes in any case, and I look forward to being contacted by the mysterious 'Anya'.

Casper Williams

PS Davina is doing much better, thanks. I'll send through the vet's report on the paw problem I mentioned as soon as I have it.

Email from Claire to Casper

Mr Williams – I have NOT been demoted, or moved sideways. I am simply not editing your books any more, because there aren't any books to edit.

And please do not consider it necessary to update me further on the health of your damned cat.

Yours

Claire Simmonds

Miss Understanding Blog
– 29th July 2010

Hi guys

I'll strangle Marley next time I see him. I went down to the gym this morning and took my iPod. Strangely enough it's the first time I've used it since Mum and Marley went home. You know how I know that? Because I climbed on the bike, hit shuffle and got an earful of the Alex Rider soundtrack. To be fair, I had told him he could put it on my iPod but the little idiot copied his CD to Dad's PC then synced my iPod to that instead of to my laptop, instantly wiping 6,753 songs, most of which I'd borrowed from friends or downloaded (ahem) from the internet. And I thought young people were supposed to be media savvy! As it happens, the Alex Rider soundtrack is pretty good to exercise to, but I'm gonna need to get Mum to send some CDs down. I'll ransom some of Marley's pants for them.

I'm super-busy at work, too. I read through Casper's file last night. So funny! He keeps sending in all these weird, stupid ideas that make the Mexican duck story look like Philip Pullman. I feel a tiny bit sorry for Katie, even though she wasn't exactly keen on the idea of taking on Casper as her author, she must be more than a little miffed that the job's been given to me, the work experience girl. I'm a bit nervous about writing to him, but at the same time I'm fascinated to see what he'll come up with next.

Also I started his book last night. It is SO good. I thought it was going to be about spaceships and lasers and things, the cover has a picture of a knobbly-looking spaceship lurking near a multi-coloured planet. But it's not like that at all. It's about this boy who wakes up in a coffin-thing on a deserted beach and has no idea how he got there. He's naked and all alone until this girl turns up and starts talking to him.

The boy asks her loads of questions but the girl is a bit vague. The boy has to work to get any info out of her and the story comes out really slowly. Casper really builds the tension, you're desperate to know what's going on but he writes so well that at the same time you feel as if it's OK to just keep reading without anything really happening. Does that make sense?

Anyway, you should all read it and we can discuss. Oh

by the way. If the author photo on the back cover is anything to go by, he's really rather dishy as well . . .

One thing I'm not too happy about is the kitchen. It's tiny and has mould on the ceiling. No one ever washes up so every time you go in you run the risk of a huge pile of crockery falling over and burying you.

According to Claire someone sends an email around every couple of weeks telling everyone off for leaving the kitchen in such a state, but no one ever pays any attention. It really is horrible in there though, you can only fit two people in at once and even then you just spend the whole time bumping into each other and saying, 'Sorry,' 'Excuse me,' 'Could I just get to the drawer there,' 'Would you mind passing me . . .' etc. I make my own lunch to save money, so eating can often be a grim business. You might think Mum's healthy-yet-tasteless-salads make for a dismal lunchtime experience, but after Philadelphia on stale rye bread four days in a row because it needs eating up, I'm yearning for Mum's Chickpea and Aubergine Jambalaya.

Speaking of kitchens, we all got an email from Mad Jack the production manager today. Claire had already warned me about him. Production people are supposed to make sure the books all get delivered on time and look good and don't cost too much. Apparently all this almost never happens the way it's supposed to. Things always end up late and look pants and cost too much, so Production people tend to stomp around a lot looking grumpy. As far as I can tell, Jack is the grumpiest by some distance. He's so odd, read this:

Email from Jack Stewart to all@Boxwood

Right you bastards.

Who's taken my grapes? I had a huge bunch of green grapes (which are NOT cheap) in the fridge and I went in there just now and they are GONE!

This is stealing. I hope whoever it is are ashamed of themselves.

I shall check again in half an hour and expect the grapes to be returned.

Jack

I'll let you know if the grapes turn up, the whole office is on tenterhooks.

Gotta go.

Love you

Anya

Email from Anya to Casper

Dear Mr Williams

Thank you for your email and submission dated 21st June which Claire Simmonds has passed to me to look at.

ow me to introduce myself. My name is Anya
delighted to be your editorial contact and I
rward to working with you.

I read your submission *Tree Hospital!* with interest. Firstly, may I point out that you misspelled hospital as hostipal throughout. You may be interested to know that Microsoft produces an inexpensive and easy-to-use spellchecker.

Secondly, after discussing with my colleagues I feel I should tell you I have a couple of minor issues with *Tree Hospital!*. Firstly, I am not convinced that children are as excited by trees as you seem to imagine. Pets, yes. Horses, yes. Trees, not so much. The absence of books involving trees is probably more due to lack of interest than to publishers not being on the ball.

Third, we were expecting a novel for older readers. *Ask Me No Questions* was of course targeted at teenage readers and we are hoping for a follow-up novel that would fit into a similar genre and age-bracket.

Third, I'm not sure tree surgeons actually perform operations on trees. Wikipedia suggests tree surgeons tend to 'use chainsaws to remove superfluous or dangerous branches'. They are not leafy versions of Rolf Harris. The illustration you supplied, though talented, seems to give the impression that uprooted trees can be operated on in-theatre. This is misleading and, basically, certain people – and I'm mostly thinking of school librarians here – might think the books are a bit of a waste of time, not to say WRONG and so probably wouldn't touch them with a barge pole.

I look forward to hearing from you with a revised synopsis, perhaps something more in line with your first book.

Best wishes

Anya Buxton

Email from Casper to Anya

Dear Ms (is it Ms? I do hope I haven't offended you by my assumption) Buxton. What a charming name, I have visions of you as some cherubic nymph dancing carefree through the Peak District with a bottle of mineral water.

I was pleased to receive your delightful letter. How articulate you were in rejecting my latest offering. I am thoroughly ashamed and have torn up my tree notebook.

I must apologize for my poor research into the field (or should that be forest?) of tree surgery. I was sure I had watched a programme on ITVHome in which trees were wheeled around on trolleys attached to drips, but perhaps that was simply an advert for a garden centre. I am also very sorry for my dreadful spelling laspses.

I sometimes wonder whether I'm really cut out for this sort of thing at all. Maybe I should look for a new job? I

good money to be made going door-to-door
people to change electricity suppliers. What
thoughts, Anya? What do you think? Writing
books? Or selling electricity? Words or watts?

I think we both know the answer to that one, don't we?
I shall call Northern Power immediately and take a
cricket bat to the typewriter.

Must go now, I need to apply Davina's ointment. Claire
has presumably filled you in on Davina's complaint?

Best wishes in any case

Casper Williams

PS What on earth is 'Wikipedia'?

Email from Anya to Claire

OH MY GOD! Claire, what have I done? He's given up
writing altogether (see attached email from Casper). I
only told him children might not be enthralled by stories
of emergency tree-bark grafts.

I'm really sorry. Shall I get my coat?

Anya

Email from Claire to Anya

Don't worry Anya, he does this all the time. He's teasing
you. The thing to do is to take everything he says at face
value. Keep working on him, you'll get there. He will not,
repeat, will not, destroy his typewriter.

And why on earth do you have a coat? It's 34°C out there.

Email from Anya to Claire

Phew! Thanks Claire. Sorry, should have realized that after reading through his file. He's certainly a handful.

Re. Coat – it was a figure of speech.

Best

Anya

Email from Claire to Anya

Ah, I see. BTW – it may be worth you trying to get him to come into the West End for a meeting. We'll probably make quicker progress face-to-face. If you can arrange it, you can use the expense account to pay for a decent meal, nothing too expensive though. Do you like Nando's?

Email from Anya to Claire

OK, I'll try.

Anya

Miss Understanding Blog Entry
– 30th July 2010

I got completely soaked on the way home. When you live in London it helps if you don't look up too much. The rule is keep your eyes down so you don't accidentally make eye contact with a nutter who'll spend the rest of the day following you around. But neither should you keep your eyes so far down that you get knocked over by a menacing hoodie riding a tiny bike on the pavement. If hoodies are so hard, how come they don't ride on the road? Pathetic.

Anyway the point is because you don't look up, you don't notice that it's just about to rain. Sounds like a metaphor for life, really. Not much else happened today, got home and ate a box of Cheerios in front of a repeat of *X Factor* with the volume way up.

I love *X Factor*. My favourite part is where the crowd boos like mad at any hint the judges might be even slightly critical of whichever overconfident wannabe has just finished an entire song without ever *quite* hitting the right note.

'That wasn't the right song for you,' shouts Louis, over the clapping which refuses to die.

'BOOOOOOO!!!!' says the crowd, realizing he's not one hundred percent behind the tone-deaf child on stage.

'I'm not blaming you,' Louis says quickly to the hopeless contestant, whose lip is now beginning to wobble. 'I'm blaming Simon for choosing that song for you.'

Clever move by Louis, now the crowd is confused. Someone needs booing here, but is it to be Louis for not showering the contestant with praise? Or Simon for choosing a song that, let's face it, was total pants?

This is what's wrong with democracy. Trying to please baying mobs doesn't always produce the best possible result, just look at Steve Brookstein. Who? Exactly.

The other thing I like about *X Factor* is the way the contestants tread this fine line between on the one hand claiming to be honest, ordinary kids from the North-East or Wales or Essex interested in nothing more than playing football with their mates and eating their mum's roast on a Sunday and at the same time making it clear they've been desperate their whole lives to escape their grim existence in Dullsville and 'make it' as globe-trotting divas. If they all love their mum's cooking so much why do they all move to California as soon as the record deal is signed?

After that I went to check my emails. Thanks for those of you who wrote in to say hi, and those of you who sent me that YouTube link of me falling into the open dishwasher at Emily's party. No I was not drunk. Someone opened the door behind me to put a spoon in, I stepped backwards and tripped over it. Could have happened to anyone. How glad am I that I wore my Bridget Jones knickers *that* night.

No emails from Al, The Boy, Jugs or Poops, though Marley sent me a joke he claims to have invented about a man who walks into a doctor's office with a duck on his head. 'It started with a growth on my foot,' says the duck.

I phoned down to Raj to tell him but he'd already heard it.

Sigh, I like living alone, I really do. But I'm really bored.

. . . and maybe a tiny bit lonely.

Love

Anya

Email from Anya to Casper

Dear Mr Williams

Thank you for your email of yesterday.

I was most alarmed to read of your uncertainties.

Research suggests it's common for writers to experience periodic bouts of self-doubt. Perhaps here at Boxwood we have been remiss in not reminding you more often of the appreciation we feel for your talent and commercial value to the company.

Mr Williams, I am currently reading *Ask Me No Questions* and can honestly say I love it. I have never been a fan of science fiction but the genre is irrelevant when one writes so well as you. I will not discuss it further until I have finished the book (the boy has discovered the nanobots can build anything he wants and he has just had them begin work on the castle) but I truly feel that it would be a tragedy were we to lose you to the no doubt challenging world of Electricity Sales.

Maybe you have a touch of writer's block? This is a common occurrence for gifted writers. There are certain techniques that may help. Please don't give up, please don't ever give up.

Yours truly

Anya Buxton

PS Do let me know next time you're in London. I'd love to take you out for a meal. Something filling, like Nando's perhaps? All on us of course!

Email from Jack Stewart to all@Boxwood

Very funny, Mr Grape thief.

I just went to check to see if my grapes had been returned only to find some smart-arse had put back the plastic bag they came in along with the twiggy bits the grapes should be stuck on to.

This is NOT acceptable. I want new grapes in there first thing tomorrow morning or else I am going to send this bag to my friend Phil who works in forensics at the MET.

Yours angrily

Jack

Miss Understanding Blog Entry
– 2nd August 2010

Hi guys

Is anyone still reading this? I guess there must be a few of you to judge by the number of hits I got last week.

Things are going well at Boxwood. The arrival of Casper Williams into my life hasn't exactly made things less mad, but it's certainly made things more interesting.

Another surprising thing happened today as well. Just before lunch, when my tummy was grumbling and the email system had just crashed and Mum was calling every thirty seconds to ask if I'd found any more of Marley's clothing and I was on the verge of slapping Katie Sniffy-knickers and jamming a tissue up her nose, who should appear by my desk but Portia. I thought she'd forgotten I was there at all, but noooo.

'Hello Anya my dear, and how are you getting on?' she said, taking off her glasses and wheezing a little as she's a bit overweight.

'Very well thanks,' I gushed. I could sense Katie looking daggers at me. She'd spent most of yesterday complaining that Portia never spoke to her. Katie sniffed pointedly and Portia glanced over at her. 'Are you coming down with something, Kylie?' she asked.

'Um no, I'm fine thanks, and it's *Katie* . . .' But Portia had already turned back to me.

'I was speaking to my son last night and mentioned to him you were working with us now.'

'Oh yes,' I said. 'How is Seth getting on at the bank?' I heard Katie take a sharp breath.

'Very well,' Portia said. 'Very well indeed. I have no idea what he does of course, it all sounds like nonsense, no wonder we've been having that recession thingie, even the bankers don't know where all the money is any more. Presumably in their own accounts – honestly the size of his bonus last year, I could hire three assistant editors for that . . . are you all right, Kylie dear? What a nasty cough. I really think you should get yourself some Lemsip.'

We waited for Katie to settle down and then Portia continued.

'Anyway, Seth is very anxious to see you again, apparently you made a great impression on him earlier in the year. Would you be free for dinner on Saturday? Seth's off to Vancouver soon so there's no time to waste. I'll have my housekeeper rustle something up for us.'

I was so surprised I couldn't think what to say for a few seconds, I just stared at her open-mouthed. After two weeks of being ignored by everyone, all of a sudden I've got myself my very own author, a posh dinner invitation and what sounded suspiciously like a date with a dashing older man.

I so wanted to glance at Katie to see her reaction but forced myself to hold Portia's gaze, now starting to look uncertain.

'I'd love that,' I said. 'What time should I come?'

'Come at seven-thirty,' she said, beaming. 'You know the address, don't you?'

'Of course,' I said, lying. Well, Mum would have it.

'Lovely,' she said and bustled off.

There was a long silence. Eventually I couldn't help myself.

'I'm off to the kitchen. Can I get you anything, Kylie? Lemsip perhaps?'

Email from Jack Stewart to all@Boxwood

Right. To the person who left a bunch of *plastic* grapes in the fridge this morning along with a note saying 'Sorry'. You are nothing worse than a thief and a crook and a scumbag. I'm going to complain to Personnel about this.

Jack

Miss Understanding Blog Entry
– 4th August 2010

Raining. Again. I've developed a technique for avoiding getting wet even without an umbrella. For those of you hayseeds who don't get up to the Big Town too often, I should explain they have these people on just about every street corner in Central London who hand out free newspapers. The papers are generally rubbish, written in the same way I write History essays – hastily cobbled together after a brief Google, full of simplistic observations and glaring typos. So unless you're *really* bored they're not worth picking up because then you've got to find some way to get rid of them. Usually I just smile apologetically at the vendors and scurry past, but I've discovered the papers make excellent makeshift umbrellas. You can walk about a hundred yards before they get too soggy and then you can just pick up a dry one from the next vendor and drop the used one back in his little crate. One of these papers advertises the fact that it has 'ink that doesn't come off on your hands', they should change that to 'keeps you drier for longer than any other newspaper'.

That's a free tip from
Miss Understanding

Email from Casper to Anya

Dear Anya

Thanks for your generous and intriguing invitation. I am on the one hand keen to meet you; I'm sure you're even more lovely than your charming emails suggest. On the other hand I am very busy at present. Let me think about some appropriate dates in a couple of weeks and I'll get back to you.

Ever yours

Casper

PS If I was, let's just say for the sake of argument, suffering ever-so-slightly from writer's block, what techniques would you recommend?

Not that I am, but I'd be interested to learn what you had in mind just in case, God forbid, it should ever happen to me.

Email from Anya to Casper

Dear Casper

Regarding writer's block, you need to get the writing rhythm back. Start by writing something other than the book. Write a letter or an email, just tap away at the keyboard and get used to the feeling of the words firing out of your fingers. At least that's how it feels for me, as though with every stroke I'm shooting tiny ideas down through the keyboard into the hard drive where they'll be kept safe for ever. Does that make sense?

Yours

Anya

Miss Understanding Blog Entry
– 9th August 2010

Dinner at Portia's on Saturday, with the beautiful Seth. Katie was totally jealous all day after I told her, so I milked it, obviously.

'Yes I got to know Seth a few months ago at a dinner party,' I said. 'Of course I had met him before, as a child, my mum is great friends with Portia, but I don't really remember him from then, he was always off at boarding school. Anyway it was lovely to meet him properly. He's so funny. He had me in stitches all night.'

'Did you give him your number, then?' Katie asked, sourly.

'No, no, it wasn't like that,' I assured her. 'Although . . . come to think of it he did give me *his* number.'

'He *what*?' she asked.

'He said to give him a call when I came to London, he didn't say why.'

'Maybe he needs a cleaner?' she said breezily, whilst pretending to type something.

'Or maybe he wants to ask me out?' I suggested firmly.

Katie sniffed but said nothing.

I had turned up at Portia's apartment building in Shepherd's Bush at seven-thirty sharp. Or at least Shepherd's Bush is where she said it was. By my reckoning it was closer to Acton Town Tube, but naïve as I am I know better than to point this sort of thing out. It's a lovely building, with a nice view out over Acton Park. Portia's apartment is ENORMOUS. It's on two floors with huge high ceilings, like those fancy New York apartments you see on the telly. She led me in to the world of chintz that is her sitting room. There were tassels on the armchairs and age-darkened oil paintings in tortoiseshell frames all over the walls. Seth was already there. He stood to greet me and smiled his big charming public-school smile all over the place. He's impossible to dislike, Seth is.

Portia asked me if I wanted anything to drink and I asked for whatever Seth was having, figuring this would be pretty safe. But whatever it was I think it must have been a double because I went a bit silly not long after I'd finished it and I found myself telling Portia about the time at school when Guy DuLancey cut a hole in his pocket, fed his willy through it and persuaded Imogen Chivers to give it a stroke by telling her it was a sparrow chick he was keeping warm in there.

Seth was falling about but Portia just looked non-comprehending. Anyway, that was the only really embarrassing thing I did apart from when I tried to spear an endive leaf and it shot off my plate and disappeared behind an aspidistra.

'Finished already?' Portia asked, peering at my empty plate in surprise.

I nodded. 'Yum,' I said.

Portia told us anecdotes about her time in publishing. I could tell Seth had heard them all before but he had the manners to look interested and laughed at the right points. 'When I went for my first interview,' Portia said, leaning across to me. 'I was about your age, you know.'

'Really?'

'Yes, the lady who interviewed me was terribly old-fashioned. This was during the days when publishing wasn't something you could make money from. It was all gentlemen paying their old school friends very little for high-brow novels and dry academic works of no interest that only a few mouldy professors would appreciate.' She took a large sip of wine before continuing. 'We didn't do much work really, drank a lot – lunches would go on for days sometimes. We never actually did anything productive.'

'Sounds like me at university,' Seth said.

'Sounds like my mum all the time,' I muttered.

'Anyway,' Portia went on. 'This lady asked me a few questions, established that I'd read and understood the classics and told me to start on Monday. "Do you have any questions?" she asked. "Oh yes," I replied, "could you please tell me what the salary is to be?" She looked at me as if I'd come from the moon. "*Salary*?" she asked. I nodded. "Well I'll have to go and find out," she said. Then she disappeared for ages. When she came back she handed me a slip of paper, as if reading out the sum was rather too common for her. I looked at it and said immediately, "Well this won't do. I can't possibly live on this."'

Portia stopped and leaned towards me to signal the punchline was approaching.

'This lady stared back at me, Anya, with a puzzled look. "*Live* on it?" she said. "My dear, don't you have a *trust fund*?"'

I laughed. She was a good storyteller.

She winked at me. 'Salaries are slightly better these days, Anya, you'll be glad to hear.'

'Not as good as in the City though,' Seth piped up. 'Smart girl like you could make a fortune.'

'Knowing me, I'd make a fortune then accidentally drop it down the loo,' I said, feeling pleased about Seth calling me a smart girl.

'Well that's where most of the so-called money made in the City goes,' Portia said, sniffily. Seth grinned at me and we shared a little moment.

After dinner we sat in the sitting room and swapped stories about the old days when Portia and Seth lived in Clifton, just around the corner from my old house. I never really knew Seth back in those days, he was usually away at school so it was strange to hear him talk about the same places I knew and loved. We even knew some of the same people.

'Do you know Jenna Hall?' he asked.

'Oh God, do I?' I snorted. 'She used to write in all the time.'

'Write in to what?' Seth asked.

'Oh er.' Well what harm was there? I didn't intend to tell him the name. 'I write a blog, I used to do this agony aunt thing, it was silly really.'

'What,' Portia interjected, 'on earth are you two talking about? What's a blob?'

'A blog, Mummy,' Seth said helpfully. 'Short for Weblog. A diary on the internet. Very popular these days.'

'A *diary* on the internet?' Portia asked in the same tone she might have used for saying 'A *Starburger* in Harrods Food Hall?' 'But surely everyone would be able to read what you're saying.'

'That can cause problems,' I said, with feeling. 'Best

not to reveal too much, I've found.'

'Then what's the point?' Seth inquired.

'Hmm?' I said, not sure how to answer that.

'What's the point of a diary if you're not telling it exactly what you think? Or how you feel?'

He had a point. I shrugged and nodded.

'This is the problem with blogs, isn't it?' he went on. 'Hardly anyone reads them. They aren't very interesting because the blogger always holds back.'

'The really good stuff is the stuff you don't want anyone to read,' I said, thinking of all the things I've written on my blog only to cut them out before posting.

'Exactly,' Portia said, after draining her glass. 'If what you're writing doesn't scare you, Anya, then you'll never engage your readers.'

I felt I should be taking notes at this point. But I wasn't going to forget this. Portia is a legend in this business; if she gives you advice, you don't forget it.

'Open another bottle would you, Seth dear?' she said, waving her empty glass at him. He took the glass and went off into the kitchen.

'There are two types of people in this world, Anya dear,' she said. 'Writers and editors. I am an editor, and perfectly happy with that. I find it challenging, stimulating and fulfilling. You, however are a writer. It is a far more difficult role and probably one that will cause much unhappiness to you and to those you love.'

She sat back in her chair and adjusted her skirt, breathing slightly heavily.

'You don't have to write, if you don't wish,' she said. 'Most writers don't write, they just dream while they get on with their lives. But if you choose to be an editor you'll find something missing, always.'

'Do you think then that editors can't be writers, and vice versa?'

'No, they can. People often find themselves in the wrong job and yet do it perfectly well for their entire lives. But deep down I think they know what they really are.'

Seth came back and poured us more wine. I didn't drink any as I already felt light-headed.

Portia saw me checking my watch surreptitiously. 'Will you stay the night, Anya?' she said out of the blue. 'There's no point you dragging yourself all the way to *East* London at this time of night.'

I caught Seth's eye and he looked away. It was a tempting offer but I was feeling hot and a little woozy and was looking forward to getting out into the cool, grey evening. 'No, really, I must be getting back,' I said. 'You've been very kind.'

'I'll walk you to the Tube,' Seth said and Portia nodded fervently.

'Goodbye Anya,' she said at the door. 'Remember what I said.'

'I will,' I said, as the lift door closed.

'Remember who you are,' I heard her say.

Seth chuckled. 'Funny old thing,' he said affectionately. I decided I liked Seth just then. He was a good egg. As we walked towards Acton Town Tube he asked me if I'd like to have dinner some time.

'I know Mum asked you to keep an eye on me,' I said. 'But you don't have to take me to dinner. I'm fine, really.'

'I'd like to,' he said. 'Seriously. I like spending time with you.'

I glanced at him sideways. What did he mean, he 'liked spending time with me'?

'Sure,' I replied. 'That'd be nice. Let me check my diary and I'll give you a call, OK?'

At the Tube barriers, he brushed my cheek with his lips and waved me goodbye. I walked down the broken escalator, wobbling a little on my heels and, with great difficulty, stopped myself from turning around to see if he was watching me go.

Hmm, I suppose this is one of those times where the blog just doesn't get the full story. Though being perfectly honest with you people, I'm not sure I get the full story either . . .

Night night everyone

Anya

Email from Casper to Anya

Dear Anya

Thank you. Your note of encouragement was welcome indeed and I'll try to do as you say – hey, I'm writing now aren't I? Maybe composing long, rambling emails to you is the exercise I need. You don't mind, do you Anya? You are my editor so I guess you'll have to put up with it even if you do. I'm sorry if I'm a trial to work with at times and I hope you'll forgive my teasing. It's just that so many editors I've dealt with are utter drones. No original ideas or thoughts, just photocopied letters coldly rejecting some concept someone's spent years working on or else identikit emails asking for the exact same thing that just happened to be commercial last year.

You're not like that, Anya.

Are you?

Yours

Casper

PS Have you ever been to Brompton Cemetery, Anya? It's quite close to where I live and I often go for walks there during the day, when it's the only quiet spot in this bustling part of London. It's stuffed full of elaborate, eerily beautiful statues of angels and saints as well as less ecclesiastical figures such as dragons and goblins. I love reading the inscriptions on the tombs and thinking about what lives these people may have led. So many of them are children. People often think things were better in the past. Every era seems to have been a 'golden age' compared to ours. But I don't think so. Not when I see those beautiful, tiny graves. Sometimes when I'm walking, I think I can still hear the quiet sobs of a mother, utterly bereft. But then it turns out to be a car whizzing by or a squirrel chattering in the trees.

I like it here, and now. I like the NHS, I like the MMR jab, I like being alive.

PPS Please find attached a synopsis for your perusal. I can rattle off a couple of chapters for you if you'd like?

Attachment:

FISHBOWL:
Set in the future, when rising sea levels have caused the flooding of large parts of London.

A boy wakes up in a hospital bed, with no memory having suffered an accident. He gradually learns he has woken into a nightmare world in which humans have become slaves to a strange race of fish creatures created accidentally by GM scientists. He is put to work in a factory, scrubbing algae from aquariums. Humans are kept in large glass tanks, sleeping inside plastic castles and squabbling over lumps of food thrown in by giant Guppy-Men.

The fish creatures drive around in big bubbles full of water and carry whips made from poisonous water plants. The boy, who used to keep fish of his own, figures out their weakness: if you overfeed them they become sluggish and lose buoyancy. He leads a rebellion but is captured and made to fight in a water-filled Wembley stadium, now renamed – The Fishbowl.

I haven't quite worked out the ending yet, but some kind of scene where he is dangling from the Wembley arch while vicious monsters thrash about in the water below should feature at some point.

What do you think, Anya, could this be it?

Yours

Casper

Miss Understanding Blog Entry
– 10th August 2010

Claire stopped by my desk today.

'Two jobs for you. Could you please email Casper and remind him his deadline is sixth September?'

'Gosh that's only four weeks, do you think he'll be OK with that?'

'He'll have to be. He's late more often than Virgin trains. He's on his last warning. If he doesn't deliver, we pull the plug and send round the bailiffs to break his kneecaps.'

'Should I word it like that? Or . . .'

'You can be a little more delicate perhaps,' she said absently. 'But make sure he knows it's the FINAL deadline.'

'Right,' I said, swallowing. 'And the second job?' Mug an old lady? I thought. Spot of loan-sharking?

'Could you take these proofs down to Marketing

and give three to Emma Turing and one to Emma Baldwin, please.'

'How many Emmas are there here?' I asked, taking the proofs and wiping some marmalade off the top one.

'Five, and three Claires.'

'How do you all know which one you're talking about?'

'Well there are the two Marketing Emmas of course, Emma T and Emma B. Then there's Little Emma in Production.'

'Oh yes, the tiny one. She's nice.'

'Then there's Birthmark Emma . . .'

'Oh, the one with the thing on her . . .'

'Yep, you know the one, and finally there's Emma-from-Sales. Not sure what her surname is, she's just known as Emma-from-Sales.'

'OK,' I said. 'I think I have that.'

'The Claires are easier,' she continued. 'There's Big Claire, Hairy Claire and me. I don't know what my nickname is but it's probably Cat Claire or Coffee-Mug Claire,' she laughed.

'Or Moody Claire,' I said, joining in. But she stopped laughing.

'Moody?' she asked, after an awkward pause.

There was a further, even more awkward pause.

'Well, these proofs aren't going to deliver themselves,' I said, and scurried off, mortified.

Miss Understanding Blog Entry
– 10th August, supplemental

Wotcha.

Thanks for the emails expressing interest in my weird little life. Fat Gareth wrote to ask if I could post any pictures of Katie as she 'sounds cute'. You obviously haven't been paying attention, Gareth, the girl's a nightmare. Yesterday she asked me if I ever plucked my eyebrows. I sometimes think I could have gone through my whole life imagining I was rather pretty if it weren't for people like Katie.

'Yes, but I try not to do it too often,' I replied. 'If you pluck, the hairs just grow back stronger.'

'If you *don't* pluck,' she countered, 'other people have to look at them.'

'OK,' I said, frostily. 'Point taken, I'll pluck tonight.'

'Thanks Grizzly,' she said.

On the other hand though, I noticed today that she's

put me in her Top Friends group in Facebook. What's that all about? Either she secretly likes me, or else she dislikes her other friends even more.

Anyway, like I said, thanks for writing in. I wasn't sure whether I should keep the blog going. I don't have loads of time at the moment as Claire has me proofreading the first six books of the new *Fairy Dragon* series we're doing. It's certainly an interesting concept. Books about dragons and fairies sell very well so the idea is to combine the two genres into one series. Genius huh?

Needless to say all the dragons are pink and sparkly and spend most of their time resolving disputes and reaffirming friendships rather than the more traditional dragon pastimes of eating virgins and laying waste to villages.

So I will definitely keep up with the blog, but to save time I reserve the right to just copy and paste relevant (and edited) bits from the hundred or so emails I seem to be sending each day, that way I'm not writing things twice. Hope that's OK. Here's the email I sent to Casper today.

Email from Anya to Casper
Dear Casper
Hello. Hope things are all well with you. Firstly, thanks for the new synopsis. It was very interesting and certainly

an improvement from *Tree Hospital!*. I definitely think this is your genre. Exciting tales of strange worlds. Having said that, I think this proposal needs some more consideration before you proceed to write a sample chapter. Firstly, 'fish creatures' seems to me to be a little too surreal. It runs the risk of looking like a spoof version of *Planet of the Apes*.

I do like the idea of a future London under occupation by malign forces though, and the waking-up-with-no-memory idea is always intriguing (if a little over-used). How about having him wake up in an unusual and possibly dangerous circumstance? Where he not only has to figure out what's going on, but at the same time act quickly to save his own life? A moving vehicle perhaps? Anyway, I think this is promising, keep working on it.

You were kind enough to ask about me. Well, things are mostly going well here, except for when I dropped a pile of costing sheets in the toilet. I was asked to help out with photocopying them before a big important meeting and the photocopier was being uncooperative. I was desperate for the loo so I went in with the report in my hand and rested it on the cistern. Then when I finished I pressed the button and knocked the report into the loo. Jack the Production Manager was furious but it didn't really make much difference because he's always like that. Sigh, Sir Alan's search continues, I guess. I think I've got away with it but I'd better not drop anything else in the loo, I reckon. If you screw up once, then that's not so bad and you can just say you didn't know better and promise not to do it again. But if you screw up twice, then you're in big trub, as Kelly Binns discovered the second time she posted nude photos of herself on the school intranet.

Apart from that I've been relatively disaster-free. Though I can't say the same for my mum. Her boyfriend Lance took her and my brother Marley to Oxford to go punting on Sunday. Now my mum, Jocasta, isn't by nature a boat sort of person. She was once violently ill on the Calais ferry on perfectly still waters and insisted on coming back on the Eurostar with a bottle of duty-free Beaujolais. But according to Marley, from whom I got the story, Lance said, 'Don't worry, I'm very experienced with boats, see. As long as you do just what I say, there won't be any problems.' That's like saying 'as long as you leave the pies alone, this diet thing will be a walk in the park, Miss Katona'.

. The idea was that they'd pack a picnic, punt a couple of miles up the river and stop at a pleasant, dappled riverbank to eat. Lance packed everything into the boat, asked Mum to hold onto it firmly while he boarded. 'Now, see, don't let go until I've sat down, Jo,' he said to Mum in his sing-song Welsh accent.

'Yes, yes,' said Mum sharply. She doesn't like being

ordered around. Lance looked at her dubiously, then clambered into the punt. At that moment, as you might expect if you'd had any prior experience with my family, Marley took the opportunity to fall into the river. Mum immediately let go of the boat, screeched, and lumbered across to save her cherished offspring. Lance hollered in annoyance as he felt himself going over. 'Jocasta, you stup—' he managed before he went under.

Marley only went in up to his knees. Lance, however, was completely drenched. So were the picnic and the spare clothes he'd thoughtfully packed. The boating trip was cancelled and they ended up having fish and chips in the car. In silence. Lance was shivering throughout, wearing nothing but an old raincoat he'd found in the boot.

There were words after they got home, according to Marley, who listened through the floorboards. Mum, presumably working on the theory that attack is the best form of defence, called Lance a silly old fool for putting their lives in danger. Lance suggested that maybe he should leave then, if that's how she felt. Mum agreed and threw his walking stick after him as he left.

'I'm sorry you had to hear all that, Marley,' I said.

'Oh I don't mind,' he said. 'Lance will be back. He always comes back.'

I hope so, I thought. It'll be tough on him if another

man leaves our troubled family. It'll be tough on Mum too. But she kind of deserves it for being an idiot.

Sorry to bore you with my personal calamities, but you did say you wanted to know more about me. My life is just long periods of boredom interspersed with brief episodes of either wild panic or hideous embarrassment.

Oh, by the way, Claire asked me to let you have a gentle reminder that the final deadline for the first draft of the second book is sixth September. It sounds like the ideas are flowing, so hope four weeks is enough to let us have at least 30,000 words.

Best

Anya

PS Claire asked me also to remind you, less gently, that this is the final deadline and I'm afraid we will definitely need the book by that date and I'm sorry to put pressure on you but, well, y'know this is like when I was late with my Economics essay and in the end I had to stay up all night, missing the *I'm a Celebrity* final and I got a cold but I DID it and you can too.

Miss Understanding Blog Entry
– 11th August 2010

Heya Blogpals.

Finally had a chance to sit and read through my emails. Lordy, you people have plumbed new depths of lethargy this summer. As far as I can make out, the most interesting thing that's happened in Allerton since I left is Guy DuLancey getting caught short after chucking out time and doing a poo in the bus shelter. If that's not disgusting enough, at least three people found it necessary to email me to say they went back to check it was still there the next day. Honestly, you people. I realize now I need to give you a project to keep you all busy. So tell me, what's the stupidest thing you've ever done out of sheer boredom? Speaking for myself, it was probably the time I cut my own hair. Have you ever watched documentaries about remote tribes in the Amazon who have this dead-straight hair in an immaculate bowl cut?

Well, when you've got lovely brown skin, ochre body paints and a lip ring the size of a pizza you can get away with that sort of haircut. I can't. Plus my bowl cut wasn't so immaculate. Anyway, knowing you as I do, I'm sure you've all done much more stupid things than that. I wanna hear about them.

This morning I overheard Little Emma from Production in the corridor arguing with Sally from the Rights department (they sell books to foreign publishers). Katie and I went quiet so we could listen.

'They're insisting on changing it,' Sally was saying.

'Why?' asked Emma. 'Why? We're due on press tomorrow. Why, for the love of God, do they want to change the picture?'

'Because they've noticed the rainbow is upside down. The red should be at the top. Red and yellow and pink and—'

'Thank you, I know the rhyme,' Emma said. 'But does it really matter?'

'They say in the real world, rainbows are the other way round.'

'And in the real world,' Emma said, as calmly as she could manage, 'wise-cracking badgers don't wear top hats. This is a book for four year-olds!.'

'I told them all that,' Sally said. 'But they still want to change it.'

'Fine!' Emma said and stomped off.

'God, I hate it here,' Katie said, as we sat down. 'They never give me any proper work.'

'Are you looking for another job?' I whispered, glancing around me.

'I can't leave now,' she said. 'I've just renewed my season ticket.'

'Is it editing you don't like, or just this place?' I asked, feeling that Katie and I might be having a breakthrough moment. Why was she suddenly being so friendly, I wondered.

She answered immediately. 'Oh both. I so don't want to work for a living. But my trust fund isn't big enough for me to stop just now. What about you?'

'Oh me too,' I answered. 'In fact my trust fund is still only in the planning stages. We've decided on the bank, now we need to think how to get the money to put into it.'

'My plan is to marry someone rich,' she said. 'Someone like Seth Bolt-Hodges.'

I looked up to find her watching me appraisingly. I knew what she was doing, she wanted to know A) whether I fancied him myself and B) whether I thought the idea of her and Seth was totally ridiculous. So was this why she was being nice to me? I tried to keep my face expressionless.

'You're really keen on him then?' I asked.

'What's not to be keen on?' she said. 'He's gorgeous, he's rich, he has a great job, he's funny, he's romantic and he has a Jaguar.'

'Yes, but is he happy?' I joked.

She peered at me curiously. 'Happy? I should think so, wouldn't you?'

'Yes, he most probably is,' I conceded. 'Look, I don't know him that well, but if the opportunity arises, I'll try to engineer an encounter between the two of you, OK?'

She beamed at me, eyes wide with appreciation. 'Thanks Anya,' she said. 'But do you really think you can do that?'

'Oh I have a lot of experience playing Cupid,' I said.

Obviously I didn't add that I always screwed things up.

Chill

Anya

Email from Anya to Casper

Dear Casper

Just a quick note to ask you if you're available for a signing on the 23rd February 2011. I realize it's a long way off but Waterstone's in Fulham is keen to get you along to sign copies of your new book. Yes, the one that's not written yet.

Hope you're keeping well. No hurry getting back to me on this, I need to head off in a sec to get back home and clean my flat. Well, it's my dad's flat (City Crash-pad as they call it on *Location, Location, Location*) and he stays there couple of nights a week, mostly to keep an eye on me I think. Anyway he's coming back tonight and he sent me a rather pointed email today asking if the hair in the bathroom sink was mine or whether someone had scalped Angelina Jolie and tried to hide the evidence down our plughole.

All the best

Anya

Email from Kirstie to all@Boxwood

Hello everyone

I'm currently in training for the Paris Marathon to be run in October. I'll be running the twenty-six miles dressed as an enchilada (con salsa!). This is all to raise money for my chosen charity – Casa de Gatos, which goes around Spain saving feral cats from a life of hunger and maltreatment.

I'll be coming around this week to ask for sponsorship. I hope to raise £1600!

Hope you can help.

Kirstie

Miss Understanding Blog Entry
– 12th August 2010

OK. Couple of interesting things happened today, one pretty good, I think and one pretty not-so-good, I think.

Firstly, Katie asked me to go out with her. She was sitting doing her eyeliner at her desk and she just started talking.

'A couple of girls from Marketing and I are going out for cocktails,' she said conspiratorially. 'Please come, it'll be such fun.'

I looked around, not sure she was talking to me.

'Erm, when's this?' I asked hesitantly.

'Tomorrow night,' she said, 'straight after work, so bring your glad rags.'

'Are you sure the Marketing girls want me to come?' I asked. 'I haven't really spoken to any of them much. I'm not even sure they know who I am.'

'Of course they do.'

'Who's the blonde one who always wears Chanel?'

'Edith.'

'Well, Edith thinks I'm the cleaner. She asked me to empty the sanitary towel bin in the loos the other day.'

'She's a great laugh.'

'Hmmm. And also the one with the fringe . . .'

'Rebecca.'

'Yes, well you know that email we got last week about challenging strangers whenever we see them because people keep nipping up the fire escape and pinching laptops?'

'Yes.'

'Well she, like, challenges me every other day. She's done it three times now.'

'She's a little short-sighted,' Katie said, sniffing noisily. 'Look, keep your thong on. I'm inviting you out for a few drinks is all. You'll never get to make any friends unless you go out and be sociable. No point sitting in your flat night after night being all miserable about not having a boyfriend.'

I blinked. I am *so* not miserable. And I do have a boyfriend, sort of. She's right about the moping around in the flat though. It was cool at first, now it's a little sad.

Not sure I totally get Katie. She's either stuck up and sniffing at me, or else she's talking like a character from the *Famous Five* – and aren't we all going to have jolly good fun! Anyway, I said yes, it means missing *Big Brother* eviction night, but I'll just have to live with that. This is real life!

The second interesting thing was that I ran into Claire in the lift at lunchtime. I hadn't seen much of her, she's so busy.

'Heard from Casper?' she asked, absently scanning her newspaper.

'Yes,' I said. Then I added, 'He's writing again, sounds good!'

I just meant that it was good to hear that he was writing, but Claire looked up at me sharply.

'What's it about?'

'Wh . . . what, the book?'

'Yes, you said it sounded good, what's the subject?'

It suddenly struck me that Casper hadn't said what the book was about and I hadn't thought to ask. Some editor I am. I think he's working on the flooded London thing, but now I think back, he didn't actually say that for definite. I didn't want to disappoint Claire though, so I blustered. 'Oh similar kind of thing. Memory loss, moon-eyed children speaking in riddles, that sort of business. He's going to give me a more detailed synopsis soon.'

'Good work, Anya,' she said fixing me with an appraising stare. 'If you pull this off . . . well, it'll be very good for both of us. Make sure you get something solid from him before the Editorial meeting next Thursday, I want to be able to go into the Sales meeting afterwards with actual words on actual bits of paper.'

And then the lift door opened and she walked out.

I swallowed nervously and followed her.

Email from Anya to Casper

Hi Casper

I don't want to distract you from your writing, but I wonder if you wouldn't mind giving me at least a vague idea what your book's about. It's just that we have an Editorial meeting next week and I need to give everyone an update. I sort of let slip the other day that you were writing again. And I may have slightly given the impression that I knew what you are writing and also that it sounded really good.

So it would be terrific if you could just put my mind at rest and give me a little 'taster' just so I don't look like a complete mullet and/or a total liar next week. Maybe we could have that Nando's meal on, say Tuesday? We could talk about it then.

While we're on the subject of writing I'm about halfway through *Ask Me No Questions*. Sorry it's taking so long, I've had so much reading to do lately that I haven't had much chance to sit and read a proper book. And what a book it is! The boy has just persuaded the girl to tell him he's in exile and is pretty much alone on the planet. He's desperate to find out more but she is ever-more evasive. She doesn't want to tell him the truth. Why not? I can't wait to find out.

If the new book is even a tenth as good as your first it will be a huge success. I have every faith in you, Casper.

Best wishes

Anya

Email from Anya to Jugs

Oh God! Look at this email I got from Casper. The boy's a nightmare, what am I going to DO?

Dear Anya

Thanks for your faith, I have a feeling it might not be entirely misplaced. I've just had a fantastic idea for a new book that I'm sure will have huge commercial appeal. You know how successful *The Boy in the Striped Pyjamas* was? Well get this – how about *The Boy in the Black Pyjamas*. It's set during the Vietnam war. A young Viet Cong boy is captured and held by the American Army. Gradually he makes friends with the son of one of the Camp guards.

Not bad, hey? I'm still working on the detail, but I think I might be onto something there.

More soon

Yours

Casper

He's really doing my head in. As is Mum – she insists on leaving her phone unlocked, and three or four times a week she sits on the damn thing and makes a butt call. As I'm the only person she ever calls it's always me who gets it. I was there in the office the other day listening to her wandering about Tesco. I kept yelling out, 'Mum! Hang up!' but of course she couldn't hear. I could just hear little snippets of her conversations. '*How* much is the tofu?' 'Are these mung beans local?' etc. She filled up my entire voicemail memory last week with her trip to the hairdresser. It was quite sweet to be honest, I was listening to her chatting with the stylist for ages and she was quite nice about me, saying how much she missed me and that. Then she started talking about Lance so I cut her off. Some things a girl doesn't need to know about her mum . . .

How're you anyway? Write soon, sweetie.

Love

Anya

Miss Understanding Blog Entry
– 14th August 2010

Well, that was an interesting night.

I went out with Katie and two of the girls from Marketing: Edith, and Valentina, who I'd sort of hoped would say, 'It's OK, you can call me Val' but she didn't. No one should be allowed to have a four-syllable name, it's excessive.

Now, I'd thought really hard about what I was going to wear. At 8.00 am I stood in front of my dad's mirror in my nightie thinking I should really have tried a little harder to find out where we were going. I texted Katie:

WHAT SHOULD I WEAR FOR TONIGHT?

She texted back to say.

SOMETHING SLUTTY, DARLING.

I didn't really have anything slutty, nor was I convinced Katie and I had the same idea of what slutty might look like. I could go with the Kelly Binns Superslag look and wear a micro-skirt and matching thong, but somehow I don't think that's what anyone's really looking for, except maybe Giuseppe from the post-room.

In the end I wore some thin black tights and a black skirt with a top from Gap that had a vaguely saucy off-the-shoulder thing going on, but only because it's slightly too big for me. I think I chose well, because when Katie gave me her customary morning appraisal she didn't sniff.

Around 5.00 pm Katie suggested we go and get made up; she pulled out a massive make-up bag, winked at me and trotted off to the loos. I hadn't the heart to tell her I'd done my make-up that morning, so I pulled out my handbag and looked to see what I had. Some cherry lip balm, a slightly bent eyeliner pencil I'd been using to write song lyrics and a congealed mess of melted lipstick from last Christmas when I'd left the bag on the radiator at Cheryl's.

Deciding that would just have to do, I followed Katie. Edith and Valentina were already in the Ladies along with enough perfume vapour to suffocate a pit pony. They were deep in discussion about some bloke they all knew, so didn't pay much attention to me dabbing cherry lip balm on in a style-conscious way then pouting at myself theatrically.

'Have you slept with him?' Valentina asked.

'No, have you?' Edith replied.

'No,' Valentina confirmed. 'What about you, Katie?'

Katie was silent for a moment as she put the finishing touches to her lip gloss. She put the tube away thoughtfully, glaring at herself before answering.

'He asked me to go home with him, but I said no,' she said.

'He asks everyone to go home with him,' Edith said, dabbing on blusher.

Claire came in at that point, rolled her eyes at us and went into one of the cubicles. No one said a word.

'Keep talking,' she called out after a while. 'I feel self-conscious if you're all listening.'

I laughed. Valentina turned on the tap.

'Thanks,' said Claire.

When she came out, I smiled and stepped aside so she could wash her hands.

'Not going to Gigolo's with this lot are you?' she asked, looking down at what I was wearing.

'Erm, I don't know where we're going,' I said.

'We might swing by later on,' said Katie nonchalantly. 'See what's happening.'

Claire fixed my eye. 'Don't stay out too late,' she said. 'And here.' She rummaged in her bag and pulled out a dog-eared business card. 'My friend Joe runs a cab company. If you get into trouble, call him and tell him you know me. He'll come and get you *tout de suite*, wherever you are.'

'Thanks Claire,' I said.

'Keep an eye on her,' she said to Katie. 'Don't go mental, I know what you lot are like on the razz.'

'OK, Mum,' Katie said. Edith giggled and Claire left.

'Don't worry,' Katie said to me, smiling. 'We'll look after you.'

Five hours later Katie was holding onto me for support on the dance floor at an awful nightclub called Gigolo's looking like she was about to vomit.

'Maybe we need to go,' I said. 'You don't look too good.'

'AhfuckoffI'mfine,' she slurred. Then she whooped and, launching herself off me, did this strange leaping dance across the floor. I looked to the heavens and returned to our table, from where I could keep an eye on her.

We'd left work at six and popped into Pizza Piazza to 'line our stomachs' as Katie put it. I hate Pizza Piazza. The tables are just that little bit too small for four people. Two people is fine, especially when you fancy the other one. But four female people with handbags, mobile phones and lip balms end up with too much crap on the table. And that's even before you factor in the many bottles of water, too many plates and at least three of those stupid little vases with wired-up flowers sticking up out of them.

Listen up, Mr Pizza Piazza Man. Fine if you want small

114

tables. Fine if you want big plates. But not so fine if you want both, OK? Something has to give. And marble tables? For why? Everything clunks and cracks and sets your teeth on edge. Sets *you* on edge. Especially when you're a bit grumpy anyway.

The others drank and I ate an entire garlic bread by myself, which made me feel better until I did the breathing-into-your-cupped-hand-thing to see if I could smell my breath, and I nearly passed out.

I felt a little out-of-place. I tried to make small talk.

'How's the new girl getting on in Contracts?' I asked Valentina, who I'd seen talking to her in the kitchen.

'OK I guess. But a little overwhelmed.'

'Overwhelmed?' Edith said. 'In Contracts? It's hardly the trading floor of the New York Stock Exchange.'

Valentina told us about a date she'd had with some guy called Lucas, who, apparently, was supposed to be meeting up with us later.

'We went to the Blind Restaurant, you know the one where they serve the meals in total darkness?' she said. 'It's supposed to heighten the other senses.'

'How did you find the food?' Edith asked.

'I just felt around until I touched my plate.'

'No, I mean how was it?'

'Oh, it was OK, except it took ages to eat 'cos I was constantly chasing peas around the plate. The waiter kept coming around asking us if we've finished. "I really don't know," I told him.'

We'd stayed there for ages while they finished off a second bottle of wine and then we'd trotted down Oxford St with all the other Friday night idiots until we arrived at the club, which was down an alley and underneath WH Smith. Then there was a lot more drinking from the other girls. We'd found ourselves a booth and made occasional forays onto the dance floor but mostly just sat there discussing whose turn it was to go to the bar.

When I got back to the booth, Valentina was where I'd left her, eating the face off this Lucas guy who they all seemed to know. I suspected he may have been the guy they were talking about earlier. Edith was also watching them, with a face like she'd just eaten a plate of crocodile testicles.

'Do you think she's all right?' I asked Edith, indicating the cavorting Katie. Edith turned slowly, she was even drunker than Katie if that were possible. Personally I'd hardly had anything. I didn't really feel in the mood, and Claire's warning had worried me slightly.

'No, not really,' Edith said finally as Katie slipped and went over. A bouncer wandered up and helped her to her feet.

'Chucking out time,' I said.

'What? No, this is Gigolo's,' Edith said. 'They don't

mind if you're slightly paralistic here. Lucas once did a little wee-wee in an ice bucket and they didn't throw him out.'

'But did they throw the ice out?' I asked, weakly.

'What? Oh yes, ha-ha. You're funny.'

I quite liked Edith actually. More than the others. She was just as shallow but she laughed at my rubbish jokes.

Lucas finally pulled away from Valentina. 'I'm thirsty,' he said.

'I'm going to the bar,' Edith said quickly. 'What do you want?'

'Beer please,' he said, smiling at her. 'And get one for Anya too, she's not drinking enough.' He had a lovely voice, did Lucas. Deep and resonant, like it was produced by Timbaland.

I stood to let Edith out and Valentina came scrambling around after her. 'Need the loo,' she said.

Oh hell, I didn't want to be left here with the Smooch Monster. Maybe it was time to go and check on Katie.

'Sit down,' he said smiling at me. I sat down. Lucas was a good-looking guy, I had to give him that. A little caddish as well. Just the sort of guy I tend to go for. I could see what the girls all saw in him.

'You're pretty,' he said. 'Anya, is it?'

The Boy used to be able to do this to me. Say something so cheesy that I should have just laughed and punched him in the shoulder but instead found myself blinking a lot and trying not to smile. Bloody men, I hate them.

'Are you old enough to be in here?' he asked, laughing.

I think he meant it as a flattering joke, like he thought I was really twenty-five and would appreciate being 'confused' with a teenager.

'No,' I said. 'But don't tell anyone, will you?'

He looked confused. Then laughed as though this were the world's best joke.

He looked about to say something else when I heard a screech from the dance floor. I looked over to see Katie being swung around by some bloke she'd collected. It was some remixed Duffy track they were playing. The sort of song where you had to swing your partner about as it's impossible to dance to. I took advantage of the excuse and went over to see if she needed help.

'You spilled my Absolut!' she screamed at her dance partner. Then she wobbled and made as if to fall. I got hold of an arm and managed to steady her.

'Right, time to go I think,' I said, pulling her away.

'OK Mummy,' she said, a little confused. I led her back to the table, seeing Edith and Valentina had returned. Valentina and Lucas were snogging again. Breathe, for God's sake, I thought.

'We're heading off,' I said. 'She's not feeling too good.'

'Are you going to put her in a cab?' Edith asked. 'She lives in Guildford.'

'That's miles,' I replied. No one said anything. Take charge Anya, I told myself. 'I guess she can stay at my place tonight, I have room.'

'Do you want me to come?' Edith asked.

'No, stay and enjoy yourself.'

Then she leaned over the back of the chair towards me, wobbled and nearly toppled over, then whispered, 'I don't want to stay and watch the Face Eating Endurance Contest over there.'

'Oh OK,' I said. 'Then sure. There's plenty of room.'

Lucas stopped snogging Valentina for a moment and gave me an enigmatic look as I waved goodbye. Edith and I manhandled Katie to the coat check then up onto the street. I made a call.

'Joe's taxis.'

'Hi, I'm a friend of Claire Simmonds. She gave me this number to call if I needed a quick cab?'

'No problem,' said the man. 'Where are you?'

Whilst I was on the phone, I noticed Lucas and Valentina had come out of the club behind us and went to stand against the wall a few shops down. They seemed to be discussing something intently. I finished the call.

'Five minutes,' I said. 'Are you OK, Katie?'

She was crying.

'You two are such good friends,' she said, between sobs. 'You're always there for me.'

'Here we go,' Edith said.

'I've only known you four weeks, Katie,' I pointed out.

'But you've been so nice to me, and I was rude to you.'

'Were you? I don't think so,' I said soothingly.

'Yes I was, I called you Grunge Spice.'

'Not in front of me,' I replied, more coldly.

'She said it to me,' Edith confirmed, grinning.

'Anyway, you're both my bests friends and I love you both,' Katie said, evidently feeling she hadn't got this message across before.

'Thanks Katie,' I said.

'OK. Whatever,' Edith added.

We stood in silence for a while until the cab arrived. We got in and I gave the exact address to the driver. But just as I went to close the door, a hand grabbed the frame.

'Budge up,' Lucas said and shoved Valentina in next to me. Then he got into the front seat.

'Erm, what are you doing?' I asked.

'Val's not feeling well,' he said. 'We thought we'd better come with you.'

The cab driver turned to look at me, raising an eyebrow.

'I don't mind Valentina coming,' I said. 'But I'm afraid you're not invited.'

'I live in Greenwich,' he said, turning around. 'Can't I just ride along with you to Docklands then take this cab home from there?'

I looked at the driver. He shrugged.

'OK,' I said.

The cab journey passed uneventfully, even though we were squashed up in the back and Katie kept alternately moaning, then singing the new Madonna single. We all piled out outside my building, Edith helped Katie inside and I paid the driver. Then I noticed Lucas had got out as well and was giving Valentina a hug. I waited for him to get back in, but he was looking up at the tower.

'Look,' he said to me. 'I'm worried about Val. Would you mind if I stayed here with her tonight?'

'Yes,' I said bluntly. I pointed at the cab, 'Your carriage awaits.'

He narrowed his eyes at me, then turned to Valentina. 'Well, come back to mine then, it's just across the river.'

Valentina thought about this. 'I dunno,' she said uncertainly.

She looked at me, as if asking for advice.

'Look,' I said. 'It's late, Valentina, you come upstairs with me and the others, Lucas, you go home.'

Valentina nodded and made to walk away from him,

but he held her arm tightly and wouldn't let her go. 'Come on,' he said.

She wavered and looked like she was going to agree for a moment, so I stepped forward grabbed her hand and pulled her towards me. 'Come with me,' I said firmly, and she nodded and came.

'Everything OK, Miss Buxton?' said Raj, who'd appeared from nowhere. He walked past me and stared fixedly at Lucas.

Lucas gave first Raj and then me a look and got back in the cab.

'Thanks Raj,' I said as the cab pulled away. 'I don't think he was going to cause trouble, but I appreciate you being here.'

'No problem, Miss Buxton,' he said. 'Have a nice evening? Other than that?'

'Yes, we went to Pizza Piazza, and then on to Gigolo's.'

'Ooh, Gigolo's, I went to a fancy dress party there once.'

'Really? What did you go as?'

'I went as a car key.'

'A car key?' I asked puzzled.

'Yes, the bouncer gave me a look like that too,' Raj said. 'He let me in eventually but as I went in he said "Don't you start anything!"' He laughed.

'Thanks Raj,' I said.

Anyway, after that everything was fine. We went

upstairs and I made everyone hot chocolate, we put on MTV and talked about whether we fancied Mark Ronson. I said he was too old and they all laughed at me.

Katie and I bunked up together in my bed (she sniffs in her sleep too) and the other two slept in the spare room. Katie had sobered up a little and we chatted for a while, still wired from the evening's excitement.

'So who's Lucas?' I asked.

'Oh God, Lucas,' she said. 'He's a designer. He used to work at Boxwood but has now gone freelance, so he pops in from time to time. While he worked there he and I had a bit of a thing, and I was . . . well, I thought I was in love.'

'But it didn't work out?' I asked.

'You could say that, and I'm so glad, because after he'd left I found out he'd also been messing around with at least two other girls in the office.'

'What a bastard!' I said, feeling this was expected of me but wondering why she was so surprised. You just had to look at the guy to tell he was a grade-A Player.

'I should have known,' she said. 'He flirts with everyone, but when he looked at me . . . ah I dunno, I just melted.'

I remembered how he'd looked at me in the bar and I had to admit she had a point.

'I understand,' I said.

'Thanks Anya,' she said after a pause. 'And thanks for not letting Valentina go with him.'

'That's OK,' I said.

'And I'm sorry about my behaviour. I know I can be a bit . . . up-and-down,' she said.

A-ha, I thought. A glimmer of self-awareness.

'Don't worry,' I said, 'it adds spice.'

'Lucas told me I'm marginally less stable than Heather Mills.'

I thought about this for a while. 'Because of the leg thing? Or . . .'

'Both,' she replied, then we laughed.

'Night, Anya,' she said.

'Night, Katie,' I replied.

Just before I dropped off I sighed happily. It had been a funny old night, but everything had worked out OK.

This morning I woke, left Katie snoring gently and stumbled into the kitchen to make a cup of tea.

'Hello Anya,' said a male voice, startling me. I spun round to see my father sitting at the dining table.

'Dad?'

'Who are all these people in my flat?' he asked, reasonably enough.

'They're friends,' I replied. 'We went out last night and I let them stay here because it was late.' I could hear myself sounding defensive, even though I had nothing to be defensive about.

'I thought I told you you weren't allowed to have parties?' he said quietly. He doesn't get angry very often, and when he does it's hard to tell, because he just goes slightly quieter than usual.

I blinked. 'I wasn't having a party. They needed somewhere to crash. Anyway, it's Saturday, I thought you were in Clifton.' I filled the kettle, flipped the switch and grabbed a cup, not wanting him to see how angry I was.

He humphed at me. 'I see, so you thought it was *OK* to have a party because I wasn't here? Is this what you get up to when I'm not around?'

'That is so unfair,' I said, hating myself for sounding like a thirteen-year-old not allowed to stay up to watch *The Wire*. 'Why are you here anyway?'

'I have some work to finish,' he said, irritably. 'I thought I'd drop in on you and see if you needed anything.'

'Well, thank you,' I said stiffly. 'That was considerate of you.' Then feeling something else was required I said, 'Look, I haven't had any parties. You just happened to turn up on the one time I've even had friends over. No boys, no drugs, no alcohol even.'

Just at that moment, with exquisitely bad timing,

Valentina walked out of the spare room, naked except for a tiny pair of knickers. She didn't see Dad, just yawned, walked over to the fridge, opened it and said, 'Fuck me. I think Lucas chewed half my face off last night. My lips feel like I've been sucking on an exhaust pipe.'

Email from Anya to Casper – Monday 16th August 2010

Hi Casper

OK, no bolloxing about this time. Forget the Black Pyjamas idea. It's a non-starter. Work on the flooded London thing. Remember what I said about the beginning, put him in a strange situation he has to think his way out of. Keep the reader guessing along with the protagonist. I look forward to seeing the full synopsis, only three weeks to go!

Cheers

Anya

PS Now that you're writing again I wondered if you'd feel happier having a fully-qualified editor looking after you, rather than me. As you know, I'm not very experienced. Please don't feel you'd be offending me if you wanted to be transferred back to Claire, or to another editor here.

Email from Kirstie to all@Boxwood

Thanks to all of you who agreed to sponsor me. I have had £46 pledged so far, so am well on the way! Unfortunately not everyone (not mentioning any names but someone in the Production Department) felt they wanted to donate to this worthy cause. I respect your decision but I don't agree that 'every second week some idiotic timewaster is running about dressed like food all the while trying to suck money out of us to save some mangy foreign animals'. I've looked back through the charity emails sent around this year so far and of the twenty-four people asking for sponsorship, only three were linked to animal charities. And not all of them involved running marathons dressed up as foodstuffs, as you claimed. One was for a sponsored bungee jump (nude) and the other was abseiling down CentrePoint dressed as an alien.

I think I've made my point.

Yours charitably

Kirstie

Miss Understanding Blog Entry
– 17th August 2010

OK, I've selected the Five Best 'Stupid Things I Did Because I Was Bored'.

Jared Freeman drank a cupful of olive oil. 'I'd got the idea in my head that olive oil was alcoholic,' he writes. 'It does share some properties with alcohol, in that it makes you vomit. But without the happy feeling.' OK, thanks Jared, lesson learned, I think.

Britney Morrison, who I don't think we've heard from before, says her friends dared her to flash her boobs at a passing train while they were waiting at the level crossing near Allerton Station. 'No one noticed,' she sniffs. 'They were all reading the paper, or watching their iPhones. Except a little boy in the last carriage who saw me and waved. I felt a bit down after that.'

'I got caught shoplifting Sharon Osbourne's autobiography,' says Grimble, with admirable honesty.

'I just resented having to spend so much money on it.' I sympathize, Grimble, but – Sharon Osbourne? Couldn't you have pinched something worth reading? 'It was a present for my mum,' he blusters. Tell it to the judge, Grimble.

'My brother and I built a flying fox across the back garden last summer,' says Willow Thomas. 'It worked really well for the first half a second then the rope snapped and I fell through the roof of the shed. I landed on a stack of growbags. We just tidied away the rope and denied all knowledge of the incident when Mum and Dad got home.' Yeah, well done Willow, I'm sure they didn't suspect a thing when they saw the teenager-shaped hole in the shed roof.

Last and very much least is Jenna Hall who says: 'I was so bored a few weeks ago that I agreed to go out with Guy DuLancey. Offensive, arrogant, obnoxious, lecherous and slightly creepy he may be, but boring he certainly isn't.' Look Jenna, there are worse things than being bored – Guy DuLancey is one of them.

Health news. I think I'm addicted to lip balm. Ever since the makeover session before I went out last Friday, I've been applying the stuff every half an hour or so. If I leave it longer I start to feel my lips drying out and I get this idea I'm puffing up like Donatella Versace in a vat of

Botox. I keep popping into the Body Shop to see their range. So far I've bought Vanilla and Guava, Avocado and Echinacea and I can't remember the third, Aloe and Iridium or something.

Write in and tell me what weird things you lot have become addicted to. Drugs and alcohol don't count.

Just after I posted yesterday's blog, when I was feeling about as cheesed-off as Victoria Beckham at a Girls Aloud gig, a shadow fell across my desk and I looked up to see the Beautiful Seth standing there smiling his You're-Special smile at me.

'Hi,' he said.

'Hi,' I said.

We smiled at each other for a while until the companionable silence was broken by Katie, who was just returning from the loo. She gasped when she saw Seth, stumbled and nearly tripped over a wastepaper basket, knocking a pile of books onto the floor as she tried to steady herself. She dropped to the floor to collect the books, affording us a clear view of her knickers.

Seth, ever the gentleman, leaped over to help, placing himself in a less observational position. As he bent over to pick up a book, Katie went for the same one and they cracked heads with a satisfying clunk. My smile broadened, perhaps this wasn't such a bad day after all.

'Sorry,' Seth said. 'Are you OK?'

'I'm Katie. I mean, yes I'm fine-OK.' She blathered, tongue flapping around her chin.

'Hello Katie,' Seth said, collecting the last of the books and taking her hand tenderly. 'I'm Seth.'

'Hello Steth, I mean Seth,' Katie said, then guffawed loudly. Then, 'I know who you are,' in a slightly creepy voice.

Seth stepped back in alarm. 'I'm just here to see my mother, the security chap said to come on up.'

'Yes. Yes, yes,' Katie ventured, nodding furiously. 'In the office. In her office.' Then she laughed loudly again. I held my head in my hands, unable to watch any more. It was worse than a Ricky Gervais sit-com.

'OK,' said Seth, smiling. 'See you, Anya.' He moved off towards Portia's office, still watching Katie, presumably not wanting to turn his back on someone so clearly deranged. After he'd gone in and closed the door behind him, Katie collapsed in her chair and slumped onto the desk.

'Well that went well,' I said. 'You certainly broke the ice.'

After lunch, when Seth had gone, I made the textbook mistake of telling Katie that he wants to take me out to dinner. She gave me a look like a gangster out of a Guy Ritchie film but better acted. I only said it to shut her up from going on about her flatmate Melia, who, to be honest, does sound like a bit of a trial. 'Melia NEVER does the washing-up. I wouldn't mind but she leaves apple cores and nutshells in all the cups.' Or 'Melia is late with the rent again. I'd kick her out but we're on this joint tenancy thing and I just know I'd have to cough up.' Or 'Melia brought a MAN back to the flat last night. Honestly, the noises coming out of her room. Sounded like she'd skinned a cat and was whipping it against a walrus.'

I waited for a break in the conversation then told her. I had fifteen minutes blissful silence and managed to read four pages of a manuscript before she said something.

'Do you think he fancies you?' she asked.

'Honestly?' I replied having thought about this very subject for about . . . oh I don't know, the last three days. 'I'm not sure. I think he probably likes me but thinks I'm too young. I think I probably like him but think he's a little too old.'

'He is too old,' she replied instantly, sensing weakness. 'For you anyway.'

'Possibly,' I replied, trying not to sound defensive.

'Definitely,' she said. 'He probably just wants to take you out as a friend, or a sort of father figure. Here you are, all alone in London—'

'I don't need a father figure as I already have a father. Who lives in the same flat as me, which rather suggests that I'm not alone either—'

'Just don't get your hopes up,' she interrupted, leaning across and looking earnestly at me. 'That's all I'm saying. I've seen it so many times before.'

'OK,' I said, trying not to roll my eyes. 'Thanks for the advice, Miss.'

Oh, why can't I keep my big mouth shut?

Email from Anya to Al

Dear Bruce Parry

Thanks for the phone call last night. I didn't mind at all being woken at 3.37 am to listen to seven minutes of crackling over the world's worst phone line, periodically punctuated with you saying things like:

Not . . . think . . . Maree . . . girlfriend . . . don . . . ha . . . all . . . sill . . . think . . . rld . . . oo . . . gotta go . . . jungle . . . ruins . . . mail . . . botch . . . love.

I'm still no clearer about anything. Have you been taking ayahuasca? I told you not to do that stuff, it makes the top of your head come off and then you vomit like Guy DuLancey did after Kelly Binns' beerboarding party. I'm not sure if you could hear me yelling back at you, but basically I'm really not happy about the fact you didn't mention Marina before you left.

Look, maybe we should just put everything on hold for now until you're back, OK? Then we can talk properly. If you get the chance, email me to let me know when your flight gets into Heathrow, maybe I can swing by and see you.

Yours

Anya

Miss Understanding Blog Entry
– 18th August 2010

Major dramas here today. Jack the grumpy Production Manager has been around shouting at poor old Katie. Apparently she added some text to all the new books to say they were printed on ethically-sourced paper from sustainable forests, when in fact she wasn't supposed to do that until next year, by which time we'll have used up all the old paper the printer bought for us. Apparently the old paper isn't in the least bit ethical. I think it's made from the skins of Indonesian children or something.

Now Greenpeace are onto us and calling us Satan's Publisher, which I think is a little harsh. Though Claire said that if Satan would like to send in an outline of his new book, together with a couple of sample chapters she'd be happy to take a look.

After Jack had gone, still muttering obscenities, Katie sent me an email:

Katie: Hate Jack. He's such a div.

Me: Why are you emailing me? I'm only three feet away. Look, I'm waving.

Katie: I don't want anyone to overhear me bitching about him.

Me: OK, but don't click on Send To All like you did with that Gary Glitter joke.

Katie: Oh God, don't remind me. ☹

Me: Please don't start using emoticons, I can see your face and you don't look sad at all. In fact you look quite pleased with yourself considering you've just had a bollocking.

Katie: That's because I've just had an idea about how you can do something to cheer me up.

Me: What makes you think I want to cheer you up? I like you when you're sad and quiet.

Katie: Ha ha.

Me: I'm serious.

Katie: Anyway, I think we should do a double-date. You and Seth, me and some loser suitable for you. Then as the evening goes on, we sort of swap over.

Me: 'Sort of swap over'? This is starting to sound a little sordid. Do we have to pick car keys out of a bowl?

Katie: I'm serious. You said you thought Seth was too old for you, you know I've wanted to get to know him for ages.

Me: Care Factor Zero. What's in it for me?

Katie: You get to meet some scrummy bloke. I know heaps of gorgeous guys.

Me: I do NOT need another man in my life just now. I'll provide my own fake date thank you.

Katie: So you'll do it? Thanks!

Me: Hang on, how did you do that? I don't remember agreeing.

Katie: Oh look, OK, if you do this for me then I promise that I'll send you some proofreading work once you've finished your work experience.

Me: Paid work?

Katie: Of course paid work. We have loads of freelance proofreaders we use to check manuscripts.

Me: That's really sweet. I'll think about it. Thanks, Katie.

Katie: No. Thank *you*, Anya.

Email from Casper to Anya

Hi Anya, thanks for your email, and for your great ideas. Yes of course *The Boy in the Black Pyjamas* was never going to work – after all, the captive wouldn't be able to speak English.

I've moved back onto *Fishbowl*. I've adapted the synopsis and am working on the first chapter now. I've put the boy in a moving car when he wakes up with no memory, but here's the catch, the car is hurtling through space and headed towards an asteroid, how about that!

But I don't want to give too much away just now.

More soon

Casper

PS How's Katie, still driving you mental?

PPS The idea of losing you as an editor fills me with dread. The idea of Claire being my editor again makes me want to leap naked in a ball of flame off the BT Tower. Please don't hand me over to anyone else. Unless, that is, you want rid of me? You can tell me straight, I know I can be a trial . . .

Email from Anya to Casper

Dear Casper

That's great news to hear you've started working on the book, I look forward to reading it. Are you entirely sure about the car-in-space thing? How would a car get into space? Surely it wouldn't be properly sealed against the vacuum? Unless it had been converted specifically for the purpose? Oh well, I suppose you must have considered all of that. Perhaps the boy's father is an engineer? The car is a secret escape vehicle built as a last resort in case the malign government's agents come around. I'm certainly excited to find out how it's going to turn out.

I know you'd rather not discuss your work too much,

but would you mind sending through the reworked synopsis now?

PS Katie's OK, though today I wore a pleated skirt with a tartan pattern on it, foolishly thinking she might like it. 'Come here straight from school?' she asked. Grr . . .

PPS I love being your editor. And when I said I wouldn't be offended if you wanted someone else, I was lying.

Best

Anya

Email from Anya to Jugs

Oh crap, that Katie's doing my head in. She's been moaning all day about how much work she has to do and she's spent three hours this morning on Facebook updating her Status every five minutes in case someone might be interested in how she's feeling today. Edith told me she's on Twitter as well. I'm not, but I can imagine what it would say:

2.29 Katie has just come back from lunch.

2.30 Katie is sniffing.

2.31 Katie is farting about on Facebook.

2.34 Katie is going for a wee.

2.36 Katie is making a cup of tea.

2.39 Katie is sniffing.

2.47 Katie is updating Facebook again.

2.49 Katie is sniffing.

2.54 Katie is moaning about work to Anya.

3.01 Katie is fighting for breath as Anya chokes the very life out of her.

3.02 Katie is dead.

3.05 Katie is sniffing.

I must have rolled my eyes audibly at one point as she looked over and said, with every appearance of sincere concern, 'Are you OK?'

'Me, oh yes, I'm peachy,' I said, trying to keep the sarcasm at bay.

'Do you have PMT?' she asked.

'Eh? No, I don't think so.'

'I do,' she said, effortlessly turning it round to a conversation about her again. 'I've been a little off my game today.'

Does she have PMT every day then? I wondered. What a bummer.

'I've got sore nipples too,' she said. I stared at her in horror and tried to turn it into a look of empathy.

'Ooh yes,' I said. 'I get that.'

'You know what I do?' she said, looking around to see if we were being overheard.

'What's that?' I asked.

'I put my bra in the fridge before I put it on. Very soothing.'

140

'Good,' I said. Then in spite of myself I smiled at her. Irritating and self-obsessed she may be, but her heart is in the right place.

Now, I must get on with reading this new manuscript Claire passed to me to read. It's called *Shuffle* and it features this boy, a thief who pinches someone's iPod shuffle. He listens to it and gets into the music but soon begins to notice a pattern in the songs. The iPod is communicating with him, telling him to return all the things he stole. He tries to throw it away, but he finds himself drawn back to it. The story gets darker as you go on, I'm really enjoying it.

Anyway, love you all

Miss Understanding

Email from Jocasta to Anya

Dear Anya

Your father tells me you had a party at his flat on the weekend and there were naked women walking around swearing and drinking straight out of the milk bottle. He said it was like Anything Goes Night round at Peter Stringfellow's house. Do you have any idea how difficult it was for me to convince him to let you stay there? He was sure you'd turn the place into a crack-den inside a week. He wanted to move Cheryl in with you – and that's still an option if you don't watch yourself, young lady. Or would you rather I came down to stay with you? Thought not.

No more parties, last chance.

Jocasta

PS Have you found any of Marley's *Ben 10* underpants under your bed? He suggests the ones in your room are most likely *soiled*, so if you do find any please wash them at forty degrees before sending back.

Miss Understanding Blog Entry
– 19th August 2010

Thanks for all the replies to my enquiry about weird things you're addicted to, here are today's Top Five:

Kayleigh Leach is addicted to Slimquik strawberry wafers. 'I'm not on a diet,' she says, 'which is just as well 'cos I ate four and a half packets yesterday.' Erm Kayleigh, don't those things have a mild laxative in them? If so, it would explain why you were seen sprinting off the hockey pitch back in April, you remember? That time we lost six–nil to Chinnor Girls College?

Saskia Garfield claims to be addicted to her boyfriend. 'I want to kick the habit but I can't keep away,' she cries. You know, Saskia, Miss Understanding would probably tell you to try another drug just to see what happens, but that would be irresponsible and glib.

Harry Trimble thinks he might as well face it he's addicted to luurve. Well, unless luurve is the name of a new gaming console, Harry, I beg to differ.

Regular correspondent Jenna Hall thinks she's addicted to my blog. Which is lovely, Jenna. Now go and get yourself a life, please.

Best of the rest is Imogen Chivers who claims to be addicted to Pringles. 'I know what you're gonna say,' she writes, defensively. 'Everyone's like that with Pringles, once you pop you can't stop and so on. But I pop more than once at a sitting. I once ate nearly three full tubes during *America's Next Top Model*.' Oh my God Imogen, you know what this means? You're a multi-popper! You need help.

Email from Anya to Casper

Hi Casper

Oh my stars, I've had the weirdest conversation yet with Katie. I was totally bored, reading some rubbish manuscript someone had sent in. Katie was annoying me. She was looking at Facebook and laughing out loud from time to time. But she was doing it in a slightly forced way, suggesting she didn't find whatever she was reading quite as funny as all that. She patently wanted me to ask her what was so funny, but I didn't because I didn't want to be manipulated. God that sounds petty now I think about it, but hey, you don't work with her.

'So what about this double-date?' she asked.

'You still on about that?' I replied.

'Do you want this freelance work?'

I shrugged and nodded. 'Why don't we make it a triple date?' I joked. 'Valentina and Lucas might be fun.'

Katie shook her head. 'No, she's on holiday.'

'Didn't she already have a holiday this year?' I said, half-heartedly trying to read my manuscript. 'She told me she went to Dubai.'

'Oh she's always on holiday,' Katie said, irritably. 'Why is it all the fun, interesting people at work always seem to be on holiday but the irritating mingers work every hour God sends?'

'Well thanks very much.'

'I didn't mean you,' she said soothingly. 'Now will you come on this date with me?'

'Who am I going to bring? I mean, who am I going to get to pretend to be your date until you dump him back into my lap? My boyfriend's in Colombia. And I'm not even sure he is my boyfriend any more. I think he might be Marina's boyfriend.'

Katie ignored this nugget of personal data as it didn't involve her. 'I'll find someone for you, don't worry. Will you do it?'

'OK,' I said, against my better judgement. 'What could possibly go wrong?'

Oh God, Casper, what have I let myself in for this time?

One thing's for sure, there's no way anyone's staying over at my place afterwards.

Anya

X

Email from Anya to The Boy

Hey you

I know you never check your email, but there's obviously something wrong with your phone, so I hope you get this. I need a favour. You said you wanted to come down for a visit? Well, here's your invitation. I need you to come down to London a week on Saturday, bring your car, you can park under Dad's building. Code to get in is 136B.

Now, you'll be going out on a double-date with a girl called Katie. My date is Seth Bolt-Hodges, Mum says you met him at that party years ago where your friend Bonkers Garth drank Portia's red wine vinegar, but I don't remember Seth being there. Now before you ask, he's not my boyfriend, in fact the whole idea of the exercise is to get him and Katie together.

Address is:

Flat 143 (14th floor)

338 Mudlark Drive

Docklands E14

Let's get one more thing straight, you are NOT, I repeat NOT, staying at Dad's flat. If he even knew you'd been near the place he'd shoot you and throw me over the balcony. You'll have to stay at the Travelodge or with one of your idiot London friends.

Anyway it would be good to see you, I suppose. Let me know if you can make it. I'll owe you BIG time if you do this for me.

Yours

Anya

Email from Casper to Anya

Hello Anya

I'm not convinced this double-date thing's a good idea. For a start I rather get the impression Seth's more into you than you're admitting either to yourself or to me and your blog. Also – don't you think someone else might be a little jealous? Your call. Just be careful out there, OK?

Can't be worse than my last date though. I asked out the girl who works behind the tills at the local Waterstone's. Well if you can't use the fact you're a best-selling author to get an impressionable young bookseller to go out with you then what's it all about, eh? We only went around the corner, to a little sushi place I like. It's one of those ones where you sit on tall stools at the counter and the tiny boxes of sushi travel round and round on a little conveyor, like a luggage carousel for gnomes. It was all going well, I was impressing her with

147

my ability to pronounce *wasabi* correctly and telling her about the book I'm working on, when I spotted a particularly succulent bit of yellow-fin tuna trundling past on the carousel. I hesitated briefly, wondering if it was rude to reach across her to grab it, but then I realized it was getting away! There was no time to lose! So I went for it. Only by this time it was slightly too far away and I was perched on the edge of the stool, so as I lunged I slipped off and bashed my chin on the counter. At the same time I got a fingertip to the box, but just caught the lip, flipping it over and spilling raw fish across the carousel.

My date appeared, on the surface, to be very concerned, but I could tell she just wanted to laugh at me. To make matters worse, no one noticed the spill so the tipped-over box and its scattered contents kept coming around again and again, a metronomic reminder of my idiocy.

Now I eat at The Noodle Bar on Lilly Rd and walk over to the Earls Court Waterstone's for my book-browsing.

Katie cracks me up. I knew someone like her once, intensely irritating, but you can't help liking them despite that. Or maybe even because of it. You'd ask her a simple question like, 'What day's the fourteenth?' and she could never just say 'It's Wednesday'. She'd have to say, 'Oh it's Wednesday, you know how I know that? Well, it's my

148

friend Gemma's birthday on the Tuesday, which is the thirteenth, and we were planning to go bowling. But All-Star Lanes have Singles Night on Tuesdays and we didn't want to go to that because you'd just have weird guys swinging fifteen-pound balls and leching off you and distracting you as you tried to pick up the spare and what if you did meet someone nice, in THOSE shoes? And so we decided to go on Thursday which is the fifteenth, so the fourteenth must be Wednesday.'

TMI, Anya, TMI.

Love

Casper

Email from Anya to Casper

Dear Casper

Hello there. Thanks for the email, but you didn't mention the new synopsis. I don't want to pester you, but Claire is quite anxious to have something on paper soon so we can start working up the advance title information sheet. I'm not going to ask how the book is going, let's just get that synopsis finalized for now.

I got an email from AWOL Al yesterday. He blabbed on for ages about some endangered tree they found but hardly said anything about more personal matters (like how much he might be missing ME) which makes me a little suspicious. I think I mentioned to you before he's on an eco-holiday in Colombia and keeps referring to some mysterious girl called Marina. I've asked him for more information and now he's gone all quiet about her. Hmph.

Also got an email from Mum complaining about a non-existent party I didn't have. Just because Dad got all hot under the collar when he saw a half-naked twenty-three-year-old dribbling milk down her front. Honestly, I thought he liked to see that sort of thing, to judge by the magazines I found in his cupboard the other day. Double hmph.

Great excitement at work today. Jonny Wilkinson was in the building. He was visiting the adult division upstairs about his new autobiography. Little Emma got in the lift with him. 'He's only a few inches taller than me,' she said, excitedly.

'You mean you're even shorter than Jonny Wilkinson?' Jack said. 'Wow.'

BTW you asked me ages ago whether I'd been to Brompton Cemetery. I haven't, but it sounds lovely. On the weekend I went for a walk along the river. I walked through the Greenwich foot tunnel and all the way down to the Thames Flood Barrier. I thought of you and your idea about setting a book in a future, flooded London, and tried to imagine what it might be like. Perhaps London would become a series of walled towns on high ground, separated by shallow reaches of brackish water.

Maybe they'd go to war with each other?

Anyway, must get on. Hope Davina's foot is better now. Make sure you eat properly and get lots of exercise. You need to look after yourself.

Best

Anya

PS How about that Nando's meal sometime? Peri-peri wings on me?

Email from Casper to Anya

Hi Anya

I'm so sorry. I've been so involved in the book that I forgot to tell you about it. It was nice to hear from you after being so caught up in writing. I knew I was missing something and now I realize it's your funny stories about breaking the photocopier, or dropping that costing report in the loo, or what mad things your eccentric mother is up to. Actually, I'd kind of got stuck in a difficult patch this morning and have been walking around in my underpants looking for inspiration. It feels good to tap away at the keyboard again. Thanks for not asking about the you-know-what. Please don't worry about the deadline, leave that to me.

So, what can we talk about that doesn't involve books? The weather? I'm afraid I'm rubbish when it comes to weather discussions. I do try to keep abreast of developments but I find it impossible. Every morning I watch the telly or listen to the radio trying to follow the reports but they just ramble on for ages about showers in Aberdeen or hail in the Orkneys and I find my attention wandering. I think about all the people in those charming-sounding places going about their lives, gutting fish or fighting off massive seabirds or whatever it is they do, and then all of a sudden I realize the weather-person is talking about London and I try to concentrate but then they've moved on to Belfast and I've missed it again. Why do they hop around the country like that? Radio 4 is the worst. They say things like, 'It'll start off sunny in North Wales and Cheshire, but by lunchtime there will be rainy spells in Kent.' How is that helpful to anyone? People in Kent need to know what's happening *before* lunch, Welshmen need to know whether to pack a picnic.

I don't know why they bother at all with the weather. My philosophy is this: Sit in the garden if it's sunny. Come inside if it rains. What could be simpler?

Don't ever feel you can't send me an email, Anya. I'm hardly swamped with correspondence. How is everyone there? How's the lovely Claire? Still single and infested by cats?

Warmest wishes

Cx

PS The thought of you covered in peri-peri wings is an intriguing one but I think I'd prefer them on a plate if it's all the same to you. Smiley face!

Miss Understanding Blog Entry
– 20th August 2010

Hello you lot.

Bit nervous about the possibility of meeting Casper. Claire said I should pin him down on lunch and then quiz him on the synopsis for his new book. What if he hasn't got anything? What do we do then? Tell you what, why don't you lot write in and give me some ideas for books? They need to be topical, edgy and a little dark. You need to give me a snappy title, a hook line summarizing what's different about the book, and then a brief synopsis of the plot. I'll post the best on the blog.

I'm also slightly bricking it about the double-date a week on Saturday. As expected The Boy hasn't got back to me about coming down to help me out. I should have known he wouldn't. Total loser that he is. So much for The Boy version 2.01, he's still the same.

So nightmare upon nightmares, Katie has said she's

going to find a date for me. 'Oh I know hundreds of lovely boys,' she said airily. 'What do you like? Rough and ready? Hard and stupid? Soft and sweet?'

'Soft and sweet,' I said instantly, which isn't true of course but I shudder to think of what Katie might dredge up for me if I asked for rough and ready. Well, it's only one night, and I have faith good old Seth would bail me out if things go badly. I'm intrigued to see how Katie is going to go about seducing Seth. I don't know him that well but I'm not convinced they'll be a match made in heaven. She's got her good points, but she's-ever-so-slightly vacant. Nor am I sure about her new haircut. She's gone and got herself one of those Betty-Boop jobs but it's all a bit overdone and I can't help thinking it looks a little like Lego hair.

Mum's finally sent me some CDs after I sent back a parcel containing some of Marley's clothes (and yes I did wash them but no, I don't want to talk about it). She was obviously in a hurry and sent down some CDs at random, so now my iPod has:

The Alex Rider soundtrack (which I'm actually starting to like).

The *Best of Simon and Garfunkel* (which I thought was a chain of restaurants).

The *Music of West Africa Vol. 3* (which Mum got free when she resubscribed to *The Anti-Capitalist*).

The *Very Best of Craig David* (which, even when compared to the rest of my Playlist, is still my least favourite, by some considerable distance).

Must get on. Need to do my eyebrows, Katie's none-too-subtle hints are starting to get to me.

Luvs

Anya

Email from Anya to Casper

Hi Casper

Nice to hear from you. Well, if it's stories about insane mothers you're wanting, you've come to the right girl. My seven-year-old brother Marley phoned me last Saturday to say Mum had somehow locked herself in the cellar, she was too embarrassed to phone the fire brigade and could I come and rescue her? He was dropping Jaffa Cakes down to her through the coal chute.

I didn't mind, because I wanted to go back for Jugs' birthday on the Saturday night anyway, but still, it took me hours to get back to Bucks. I could have cadged a lift with my dad who was working that day but we had a little falling-out so I didn't fancy the idea of spending an hour and a half listening to him think of new ways to make me feel guilty. When I got home, Marley was asleep with a pillow and blanket against the cellar door and I could hear Mum's gentle warbling on the other side as she sung him the *High School Musical* soundtrack. I rescued Mum, put Marley to bed and went up the hill to see Jugs, but by then I was so tired I went to sleep in The Bull and they just left me there in the snug, snoring gently.

Sometimes I worry for Marley, but he loves living with Mum so much, he really doesn't like it when he visits Dad and Cheryl. And sometimes she can be just the best mum in the world. I guess living in our household is high-risk, high-gain. I do wish Jocasta wouldn't fill his head full of horror stories about global warming though. He phoned me up the other day to ask my opinion.

'What's going to happen when the sea floods our house?' he asked.

'Don't worry about it,' I said. 'Our house is a long way from the sea.'

'That's easy for you to say,' he pointed out. 'You're really tall. I'm only little so I'll drown first.'

'Really Marley, don't worry about it,' I said in a reassuring tone. 'You can stand on a chair.'

You asked about Claire, she's very well and yes, still single. I do like her, she's half-heartedly looking for romance, but says her real interests in life are Persian cats and subjunctive clauses. She's quite happy with the idea of growing old, sending strident emails to the *Guardian's* corrections and clarifications column and eventually being eaten by her cats. 'If all I have to offer the world are my skills as a sub-editor and fifty-five kilogrammes of lean flesh, then so be it,' she said to me the other day.

I've been in trouble with the folks. It wasn't my fault, I had to put some friends up in an emergency (I was saving one from a fate worse than death) and my dad turns up the next morning and assumes I'm having a party.

Anyway to cut a long story short, I'm on my last warning. If I'm caught with unauthorized people in the flat again, one of the oldies will have to come and stay with me as chaperone. Either Dad, Mum, or worst of all, Cheryl, Dad's new wife. It's not that I don't like her, but we have history and it'd just be too awkward.

Anyway, enough of me rambling on, hope you're eating properly and not spending all the hours in front of that PC. Has Davina's rash cleared up fully now?

Anya

PS – Yes, plate of peri-peri wings perhaps more appropriate for a business lunch. Will make mental note.

PPS Are you aware you actually wrote the words 'Smiley face' at the end of your last email?

Email from Anya to Al

Dear Ray Mears

Imagine my surprise this morning when I checked my inbox to find NOT ONE email from you. I appreciate you're trekking through the jungle searching for the source of the Amazon or whatever and have had to carry the gorgeous Marina most of the way ever since her bra-strap broke, but come on! South America is chocka with backpackers eager to email home and download hundreds of samey-looking pictures of rare trees. Internet cafés are the third largest source of foreign income for Colombia, after ransom payments and cocaine. I find it very hard to believe you couldn't have found your way to sending me a quick note to let me know you're alive and haven't been kidnapped. Hmph!

BTW – if you *have* been kidnapped, could you make it clear to your captors that I am totally skint. I could probably scrape together £25 if absolutely necessary, but any more than that and you'll have to wait until Dad comes over on Thursday.

Yours grumpily

Anya

Email from Casper to Anya

Dear Anya

It's good of you to think of me. Even if it's just a professional interest you are taking.

Your mother sounds wonderful. I know you find her terribly frustrating at times, what daughter doesn't? But you must count your blessings. When we're tiny we think our parents will be there for ever, don't we?

I've been reading your old agony columns, they're hilarious. I understand why you wanted to stop, but I sometimes feel I could do with some advice on my love life, or on how to get one. There's this girl in my gym, for example, who I quite like the look of, and I think I've seen her looking at me too. I first saw her about six months ago and since then she's lost loads of weight, and looks really amazing. Now the question I'd put to Miss Understanding is: should I tell her? I mean, is it weird to approach a girl in the gym and tell her she's lost weight? Will she think I've been checking her out for ages like some kind of step-machine stalker? I'd appreciate any advice you might have.

Say hi to Claire for me, won't you? I did give her a hard time when she was my editor, I'm much nicer to you. I suppose you've charmed me, eh? Claire's plan to offer her flesh to her cats is indeed a noble sentiment. Speaking for myself, I'm also convinced I'll end my days alone. I suspect I'll end up as one of those old men you see in the gym changing rooms who spend hours undressing, swim for eight minutes, then spend the rest of the morning putting their clothes back on.

Anyway, no point being downbeat, I'll save that for the book. On a brighter note, I need to pop into town on Tuesday on a couple of errands. Thought I might take you up on that offer of a lapful of peri-peri wings.

Nando's, did you say? Around one-ish?

Yours

C

PS Just a business lunch, of course. For discussing business matters only.

PPS I know I wrote 'Smiley face'. It's just that I find emoticons so naff but I wanted to let you know I was only joking about the peri-peri wings. I know I'm ridiculous. Embarrassed face.

Miss Understanding Blog Entry
– 20th August, supplemental

Heya.

Lucas was in the office today, dropping some artwork off and basically making a nuisance of himself, wandering around and flirting with all the girls. I was sitting in the Production meeting when he walked past and gave this really creepy wink which everyone saw. Katie reckons he fancies me, but there's only one person that boy fancies and that's himself.

I ran into Jack in the kitchen afterwards. 'You want to watch that Lucas,' he said. 'He's really weird.'

'In what way?' I asked, pouring myself a coffee.

'He pulls down his trousers at the urinals,' he said.

'Is that not normal?' I asked. 'I don't really know what you lot get up to in there.'

'Of course it's not normal!' he said. 'You're supposed to keep your trousers up, and just pop it out of your fly.

Lucas actually drops his trousers and stands there, butt-naked, while he pees.'

'OK,' I said.

'And another thing,' Jack went on. 'Sometimes he stands there for longer than he needs to. You know, to make it seem like he's got a bigger bladder than you.'

'Thanks for the insight,' I said, wishing I hadn't asked.

'Like I said, he's weird,' Jack finished, then walked off.

'You're weird too,' I muttered, after he'd gone.

Email from James Buxton to Anya

Anya, I went back to the flat for lunch today with a colleague and was mortified when my colleague sat down on the couch only to find he'd sat on a clump of used leg-waxing strips. *Please* could you make more of an effort to keep communal areas clean and tidy? I don't mind what you get up to in that sinkhole of a bedroom of yours. When you move out, I'm getting professional cleaners in.

Oh, and why is there a bra in the fridge? I've left it there in case there's some important reason but want it removed by the time I get home tonight.

Yours

Dad

PS I've left some money on the counter in case you want a takeaway.

Email from Anya to Casper

Hi Casper

Regarding your gym conundrum, I've asked Miss Understanding, and she had this advice:

Dear Casper

The thing is, whilst she's body-blasting, or butt-crunching, she's probably not looking her best, what with having a red face and a sweat-sodden gusset. So she might not appreciate your advances then and there. On the other hand, the whole point of her going to the gym is that she's trying to look nice and would probably appreciate someone making the effort, as one gym-rat to another, to give her some positive feedback.

I say go for it. But try and catch her after she's showered. Though don't, of course, go into the ladies' showers to wait for her. And don't stand just outside either, that's a bit weird. You need to bump into her 'by accident', though without actually making physical contact. And don't kick off with, 'You used to be really fat, now you're not so much.'

OK?

Love

Miss Understanding

Anya here again. So yes, 1.00 pm at Nando's (the one on

Frith St in Soho) on Tuesday sounds perfect. And yes, of course, all entirely, completely business. If I start nattering about anything not businessy then I shall understand if you dash a drink in my face and walk out. Winking face.

Ax

Miss Understanding Blog Entry
– 23rd August 2010

Thanks for all your great suggestions for Casper's second novel. I'm not sure any are usable, but I've included the less obscene ones below. Enjoy:

Doghouse! by Blingrrl.

It's a dog-eat-dog world in Broken Britain 2020.

Britain is full of bad dogs, everyone walks around with vicious canines for protection or intimidation. Gangs of youths run with savage mutts. The government has built giant super prisons specifically for dogs and gives people a choice: they can see their bad dogs put down, or they can go into prison with them! Many choose prison. Inside is a dog-eat-dog world, and a dog-eat-man world, and a man-eat-dog world. You get the idea.

Very good Blingrrl, *Dog Borstal* with teeth!

Jenna Hall writes in with the following idea, which to me sounds more like a TV series than a novel. A good TV series mind you, I think you should pitch it to ITV, Jen.

Re-Branded! by Jenna Hall
In which controversial sex-addict Russell Brand wakes up to find himself in the body of comedienne Jo Brand, and vice versa. Though initially shocked and dismayed, they each soon grow to appreciate the other and learn lots about themselves in the process. In particular, they are both pleased they don't really have to do anything different with their hair.

Bad Fairies by Trina
Similar to other fairy series, but in which the fairies smoke, play truant and steal each other's boyfriends. Like *Gossip Girl*, but with glittery wings.

Hmm, bit short on the description there Trina, but I guess what else is there to say?

It was a brave effort from you all. It's harder than you think, isn't it, coming up with clever ideas? You have to be clever, for a start. Which counts me out.

Got myself a new lip balm today. Tangerine and Essence of Artichoke. I'm loving it but this lip balm thing is getting serious. My handbag is now so full of little pots I can hardly close it.

This can't go on! I'll have to get a bigger bag.

Love

Anya

Email from Anya to Claire

Hi Claire

My God, Casper wants to have lunch with me tomorrow, at Nando's. This is a good sign, surely?

Anya

Email from Claire to Anya

Hi Anya

Hmm, don't get your hopes up. Gnawing corn on the cob is one thing, typing 100,000 words of a prize-winning story is another. Just get that damn synopsis. We need to know he's not wasting his time writing a pile of crap.

But well done and fingers crossed. I need you to single-handedly re-engage him in the publishing process. Wear something attractive, yet businesslike. Tie your hair back and don't overdo the foundation.

Oh and I have some tweezers if you need to borrow them.

Cheers

Claire

Email from Anya to Claire

Hi Claire

OK, I think I can do all that. Shopping trip tonight.

Just one question, is there something I should know about Casper's parents? He's a little wobbly when the subject comes up.

An

PS And don't you start on the whole tweezers thing, you're as bad as Katie. I'll do them tonight, OK?!

Email from Claire to Anya

Hi Anya

Oh didn't I mention? Casper's parents died in a car crash when he was five. His grandfather brought him up but died a few years ago. Casper's been pretty much alone in the world since. Perhaps that explains part of his oddness. Sorry I should have mentioned it. Best to avoid talking about families with him altogether really.

Claire

PS Um, sorry about the tweezer comment.

Miss Understanding Blog Entry
– 24th August 2010

'Every now and then you should get off with someone considerably less attractive than you,' Katie said to me today as she flicked through a magazine.

'Er . . . what?' I said. I'm getting good at ignoring Katie when she witters on, but sometimes she says stuff you just can't let by. 'Why?'

'You've got to give a little bit back,' Katie said flipping past the book reviews to get to the Fashion Features. 'Y'know, make someone's day. Haven't you heard about that Random Acts of Kindness movement? You've got to give something back, pass it down.'

'Yes, but that means buying someone a cup of coffee, or helping an old lady across the road,' I pointed out. 'Not showing your pants at a *Star Trek* convention.'

'I'm just *saying*,' she said.

What she was saying worried me a little, but I couldn't

quite work out why for a while, then I got it.

'Does this have something to do with this double-date?' I asked.

'Hmm?' she said, pretending not to listen.

'Look,' I said. 'I'm still hoping my friend The Boy is going to turn up and help me out, but on the off-chance that you DO need to come up with someone for me, then no mingers OK? I know it's not a real date but I have standards even for fake-boyfriends.'

Katie just sniffed and pouted a little. 'Anyway,' she said. 'I don't think you should have invited your precious Boy. You shouldn't let him meet Seth. Keep boyfriends apart.'

'Neither of them are my boyfriend, that's the whole point.'

'Just saying that crossing the streams is a bad idea.'

'Look,' I went on. 'It's got to be believable. Seth's going to be suspicious if I "dump" him halfway through a date so I can go off with whatever Chelsea munter you've managed to dredge up for me.'

'OK!' she said. 'Whatever.'

There was silence for a while, broken only by the sound of her flipping pages irritably.

'Out of interest,' she said finally. 'What level of attractiveness would you say is appropriate for you?'

'What unit of measurement are we using?'

'Actors.'

'So at the top would be Josh Hartnett and the bottom might be . . .'

'Verne Troyer, you know, Mini-Me from *Austin Powers*?'

'OK,' I said. I thought for a while, then said, 'I'd be looking for a . . . Jake Gyllenhaal.'

'What?!' she cried. 'Are you joking? You couldn't get Jake Gyllenhaal.'

'I must have misunderstood the nature of the exercise,' I said frostily. 'I thought you were using actors as a unit of measurement to decide what level of attractiveness I was looking for in my fake date. I didn't realize you were asking me if I thought I could get a famous actor to snog me.'

'I'm just saying you couldn't get a Gyllenhaal,' she said primly.

'Neither could you,' I countered, disappointed in myself for descending to her level.

'I could get Leonardo DiCaprio,' she said.

'Hah, James Corden maybe,' I said.

'You could maybe get Minty from *EastEnders* if you did your hair,' she suggested. 'Or maybe Billy Mitchell.'

'This is stupid,' I said. 'Just make sure he's not a minger.'

'Fine,' she said and went off to the loo, leaving me fuming.

We had a Sales meeting before lunch. First we looked at some covers. Based on the vague synopsis I'd put together, Design had done a cover for Casper's new book. It was an image of post-apocalyptic London inside a giant fishbowl with menacing-looking spaceships hovering over, dropping in coloured flakes which were exploding over the Gherkin building.

'Perhaps slightly too literal?' suggested Claire. But the Sales people seemed to like it.

'Can we get a new author photo?' Asked Emma B. 'Could we not get Casper to smile a little?'

'I don't think I've ever seen Casper smile,' Claire said.

'Take a picture of him when he gets his next big cheque,' said Clive, the Financial Director.

Later we discussed what topical issues our target audience was interested in. I wasn't really following, to be honest, I was too busy worrying about Casper's non-existent manuscript and wondering whether you could get fired from work experience.

'What are your thoughts, Anya?' Claire said to me out of the blue.

'Hmm? Wazzat?' I said, wondering why she was picking on me.

'It would be good to get a perspective from someone close to the target audience,' she said. Katie cleared her throat.

'Well,' I began. 'I suppose we young people are interested in green issues?' It was a bit limp. 'Green issues' is the go-to option here.

'Not the students who live next door to me,' snorted Jack. 'I've told them a dozen times you can't put pizza boxes in the recycling bin. They've started dropping them over the fence into my wormery instead.'

Claire looked slightly disappointed with my response. I had to come up with something else.

'Actually that's a good point,' I said. 'It's perhaps true to say many teenagers aren't as interested in green issues as most adults seem to think.' Claire raised her eyebrows and waited for me to go on.

I shrugged. 'My mum's a lot more into saving the planet than I am, and most of my friends have the same sort of half-hearted approach I do. We get all PC when we're discussing it in school, and everyone's very quick to blame past generations, but when we're offered the chance to fly to Ibiza at half-term we kind of forget to save the planet for our future children.'

'And our children's children,' Katie added, helpfully.

'That's very interesting, Anya,' said James, the Sales Director, making a note. 'That certainly accords with my experience. My daughter seems to have all the time in the world to go on marches about environmental issues but never has time to stop and turn off a light when she leaves the room.'

There was much tutting and grumbles of assent from all the parents of teenagers in the room.

'And as for my little brother,' I said, warming to the theme, 'his idea of saving water is not washing his hands after using the loo. Or flushing.' Everyone laughed and I couldn't help smiling.

'Thanks, umm, Anya,' James said. 'Now, moving on to the new *Fairy Unicorn* series, books thirteen to eighteen . . .'

I sat back and Claire winked at me. Maybe I'm not so bad at this job after all.

More later, off to meet Casper for lunch, he'd better have something for me . . .

Love

Miss Understanding

Email from Sandra to all@Boxwood
Has anyone left some lip balm in the ladies' loos? It's a little tub, about three-quarters full and is Plum and Kidney Bean flavour.

Email from Anya to Casper
Hi Casper
Oh God, did I get the wrong Nando's? I waited for nearly an hour. Then I asked them to phone some of the other

branches. I meant the one on Frith St. Were you somewhere else? I don't have your mobile. I'm so sorry if I screwed up. Hope you're not annoyed.

Worried

Anya

Email from Anya to Casper

Hi Casper

Hello? Did you get my email?

Anya

Email from Giuseppe to all@Boxwood

Dear all

Who taking the wire basket from my post trolley? How the hell I supposed to delivering the damn post without the bollocks basket? Am I supposed to carry every piece of post one by fucking one?

If anyone see it, please to email and let me know.

Giuseppe

Post-room

Email from Anya to Seth

Hi Seth

How are things? It was lovely to see you at Portia's the other night. Thanks for the dinner invitation for Saturday, but would you mind if we made it a foursome? My friend

Katie has a date with a new guy and she's not sure about him and has asked me for some moral support.

Hope that's OK, and are you sure you want to pick me up? I'm happy to take the Tube.

Best

Anya

Email from Anya to Casper

Hi Casper

I hope everything's OK. Once again, sorry if I messed things up. I seem to be messing everything up at the moment. When Claire came in this morning she looked a little red-faced. I asked her if she was OK.

'Oh yes,' she said, smiling warmly. 'Rode my bike in this morning, trying to save the planet, you know.'

'Oh right,' I said. 'That would explain the bad case of helmet hair you have. Ha ha.'

'I didn't wear a helmet,' she replied, her smile cooling somewhat.

'Oh in that case it looks fine,' I lied. After an awkward pause she went into her office and Katie nearly split a side laughing at me.

Anyway, enough about me, please get in touch, won't you?

Best

Anya

Miss Understanding Blog Entry
– 25th August 2010

Oh bloody hell, I've really gone and done it this time. I arranged a business lunch yesterday with Casper. We'd had a lovely email chat the other day. He was charming (and I thought maybe even a little flirtatious!) and everything seemed fine.

Except he didn't show up!

He blew me out!

He stood me up!

My first thought was that I'd got the wrong place, but I'm sure I didn't. I definitely said Frith St. So I checked the sent emails on my laptop, and I definitely told him. Then I wondered if he'd shown up, taken one look at what a giant minger I am and hoofed it. I was nearly in tears as I left the restaurant. I phoned my boss, Claire, to tell her about it, but she wasn't there. I spoke to Katie instead.

'Oh God,' she said, 'I *told* you to do your eyebrows.'

'Thanks Katie, that helps a lot.'

'Look, don't worry about it,' she said. 'Everyone knows Casper Williams is flakier than a sunburned croissant.'

But I am worried. Not just because I thought I'd actually made a connection with him, but also because he *is* flaky. He's vulnerable. I'm worried something terrible has happened.

What should I do, guys? What should I do?

PS And it's my birthday tomorrow – this sucks.

PPS Got my lip balm back from Sandra though. So that's something. Picked up a nice Chapstick today as well from Superdrug – musk-scented. Mmmm.

Miss Understanding Birthday Special
– 26th August 2010

What a crap birthday. Got up and checked my email first thing. Nothing from Casper, nothing from Al. A rubbish last-minute e-card from Jake and Crumpet. Nothing from The Boy of course and nothing, NOT ONE THING from either of my so-called parents.

I did get an email from Seth, though he doesn't know it's my birthday of course. He was just emailing to confirm it was OK for me to bring Katie and A.N. Other on Saturday. I'm still not sure whether he thinks we're having a proper date or whether he's just been instructed by Portia to look after me in an avuncular sort of fashion. I'll assume the latter unless he kisses me. If he does that I'm not sure what I'd do but I'm not crossing that bridge yet.

Nor has anyone phoned today. Still, I suppose it's only 10.15 am, should give them a few more hours before I phone anyone in a blubbering rage. I've dropped numerous hints over the last week or so that today is my birthday, but if Katie picked up on it she's decided not to say, or do anything. I wasn't exactly expecting balloons and teddy bears adorning my desk when I came in this morning but a card would have been nice. I realize now I made a tactical error telling Katie when my birthday was. If I'd told Edith, or Claire, or even Giuseppe I'm sure word would have got around and one of the mumsy ones in the Sales department would have baked me something.

Sigh . . . no sign of any Topshop vouchers either, which is what I've been asking everyone for for about, oh I don't know, a year? Sigh, must do some work, more later.

Yours

Anya

Miss Understanding Birthday Blog
– 26th August, supplemental

Right, still no email from Charley Boorman, over there in Colombia. He can't even be bothered to send me an email on my birthday. Does this mean I'm officially, as well as effectively, single? Do I want to be single? Oh who knows? Hey, you do! Write in and tell me what's good about being single, I'll post the best five in a few days.

It's now afternoon. Katie got my hopes up by suggesting we go to the pub for lunch. Maybe she's organized a surprise party, I thought momentarily. But no luck. She just needed my help trying to organize her own birthday party next month. I say she wanted me to help, she actually just wanted me to suggest things that she could screw her face up at and disagree with.

Her: 'I don't have an enormous budget. Do you think I should just put a few hundred behind the bar?'

Me: 'Yes, that would get everyone in the mood.'

Her: 'But then the drinkers would just get drunk, at my expense and end up making the non-drinkers feel uncomfortable.'

Me: 'Oh OK, well how about spending the money on food instead?'

Her: (Looking at me as if I'd just arrived from the moon.) 'Have you *seen* my friends?'

Me: 'No.'

Her: 'Well, most of them don't eat at all.'

Me: 'Well, just get a few bottles of wine for the drinkers, some canapés for those that do eat, and spend the rest on a DJ.'

Her: 'A DJ? This isn't a provincial wedding. There'll be no *Macarena* or Chumbawumba at my party, thanks very much.'

Me: 'Then just book a cool venue and spend the money on a nice new dress for yourself.'

Her: (Giving me a withering look.) 'That's a little selfish, don't you think?'

Me: 'I suppose so.' (Pause.) 'What about a puppet show? Ha-ha.'

Her: (Ignoring joke.) 'I think I'll do party bags. With CDs and miniatures.'

Me: 'That sounds like a good idea.'

Her: 'Yes.'

When we got back Claire snapped at me for talking too

loudly outside her office while she was on the phone.

Still no word from Casper. We have an Editorial meeting tomorrow and Claire's expecting the final synopsis for the book. Looking back through my correspondence with Casper, I'm not entirely sure he's working on the book I think he's working on. He's very good at giving you the impression he means one thing without actually saying so. I've decided I'll have to write the synopsis myself.

Oh bollocks. I've just realized there's only eleven days before Casper's due to hand in the manuscript. I hope his silence means he's working on it twenty-four hours a day. Somehow I doubt it. Maybe I should just write the book myself. I'm not really very good as this editing lark. Maybe I should apply for that job in Contracts instead . . .

This is a rubbish birthday.

Love

Anya

Miss Understanding Blog Entry
– 26th August, supplement to supplemental

And I'd thought it couldn't get any worse. I've just realized I've lost my bag! Or maybe it's been stolen. I must have left it in the pub we had lunch in. Usually I just take my purse because I'm so good at losing things, but I need my lip balms, you see. So I've been taking it with me everywhere. Now I've lost it! I still have my purse, so it could be worse, but I've lost my iPod, my phone, some random photos of Crumpet and Jake at Chessington, three or four packs of tissues and about half a ton of lip balms. Who'd want to steal that pile of crap?

I ran back down to the pub but I couldn't see it anywhere. The girl behind the bar said she'd keep an eye out but she didn't seem to share my concern as much as I would have liked, I guess people lose bags there all the time.

This is the worst birthday ever.

MU

Miss Understanding Blog Entry
– 27th August 2010

I love you, I love my family. I love everyone. What a great birthday!

When I got home, feeling about as happy as Louis Walsh discovering he's got the Groups again, I shut the door and nearly fell over when I saw Jugs sitting on the couch watching *The One Show*.

'Hey Bird,' she said. Then she couldn't keep up the casual act and rushed over to give me a hug. 'Happy birthday,' she said.

'You got the night off!' I said.

'Of course I did, you idiot, I wouldn't miss your birthday. Now get ready, we're going out.'

As I was getting ready, already pretty excited, the phone rang and it was the pub where I'd had lunch. It was the landlord who said he'd found a bag and maybe it was mine.

'I asked the girl,' I said, 'and she told me there hadn't been any bags handed in.'

'Oh her,' he said. 'She's useless. Now let me describe the contents of the bag and you can see if it's yours.'

'OK.'

'One pink iPod nano.'

'Check.'

'One extremely small mobile phone.'

'Check.'

'One Cherry and Guava lip balm.'

'Check.'

'One Tangerine and Essence of Artichoke lip balm.'

'Check.'

'One Chapstick: Musk.'

'OK, I'm going to stop you there. It's definitely my bag, OK? That Chapstick's a limited edition and there can't be more than a dozen in London.'

'OK,' he chuckled. 'Well, it's behind the bar if you want to come and collect it. Ask for Gary.'

'Can I pick it up on Monday?'

'No problem.'

Twenty minutes later Jugs and I were in the lift. I was scrubbed and plucked and taking a risk by wearing the James Blunt T-shirt I was never quite sure people would realize was ironic.

'Where are we going?'

'You'll see,' she said.

It was a lovely evening and we walked a block or so towards Canary Wharf chatting about nothing. I realized earlier in the year that Jugs is the person I can just be myself with. I don't have to be understanding, or clever, or funny with her. I can just talk rubbish and veg out and not say anything if I can't think of anything worth saying. I think she'll be my friend for always because of that reason. Someone I can not see for a year, then when we do meet up we can just slip back into the comfortable way we have with each other.

'How's the love life?' I asked.

'Don't go there!' she said.

'Oh, I'm going there, all right.'

'Really, don't go there!'

'I *am* going there, and I'm taking a tent.'

'Well, you'll be camped out for nothing because I honestly have no love life,' she sighed. 'Unless you count my developing relationship with Cadbury's Dairy Milk. What about you?'

'Don't go there!' I said.

'How's Al?'

'Al is . . . absent,' I said. It was strange, but when Jugs asked me how my love life was, Al wasn't the first boy who popped into my head.

We went up the escalators into the eastern end of the

Canary Wharf shopping centre. I turned around to face her. 'Trust game?' I asked.

'OK,' she said, peering around me to see. If you haven't played it, the trust game involves standing backwards on the escalator, or moving walkway, and trusting the other person to tell you when to turn. If you look first you lose. If you fall on your arse you both lose. No trust!

'So what's new?' I asked, trying to change the subject from boys.

'Not a lot,' she said. 'Other than work. Oh, except I'm taking swimming lessons. *Now!*'

I spun around just in time to step neatly off the top step.

'Cool,' I said. 'How's that working out?'

She shrugged. 'OK, sort of. My coach says I'm doing everything properly and moving my arms and legs right, but I never seem to actually be able to move forward.'

'Maybe you should get in the water first,' I suggested.

'Ha-ha,' she said. 'Actually I have good buoyancy, I've been told.'

'I can see that for myself,' I said. 'They're getting bigger by the week, like twin airbags from a Ford Mondeo.'

'They're not that big,' she said looking down at her chest.

'OK, twin airbags from a Nissan Micra,' I said.

'Thank you,' she said, satisfied. 'Anyway, I haven't had

any complaints.'

'Heard from The Boy?' I asked, regretting it immediately. That sensitivity class really paid off didn't it? If you haven't heard, I recently walked in on Jugs and The Boy having a snog, and it's a bit of a sore point.

To her credit, she didn't react badly.

'Yes, apparently he's getting on fine up there in Doncaster.'

I snorted, but wasn't quite sure why. Somehow the thought of The Boy settling down into a nice, safe existence seemed . . . well, wrong. Like Pete Doherty winning Eurovision. There was no time to pump her for more information as we'd arrived at our destination, which turned out to be Carluccio's near where my dad works. Jugs led me in.

'Anya!' I heard and a small figure hurled itself forwards and knocked the wind out of me.

'Hello Marley,' I wheezed. 'What are you doing here?'

But it wasn't just Marley. Mum was there, and Lance and Dad and, get this, Cheryl, sitting as far away from Mum as possible.

'A Bucks posse,' I cried, delighted. 'You've all come to see me.'

Then they sang Happy Birthday, which was embarrassing but bearable, and I couldn't stop grinning all the way through it, I was just so pathetically grateful

191

to see them and so pleased that my birthday wasn't to end with a tin of beans and back-to-back *Glee* on dvd.

Dad had got us champagne so we drank a toast and settled down, discussing the menu in great depth, Mum complaining that the writing was too small and Cheryl asking everyone if they thought the chef would mind doing her cheese on toast for a starter.

She's so fussy, Cheryl. And not just fussy, but she's very vocal about what she likes and doesn't like. If she likes something it's 'THE best food in THE World like, ever.' If she hates something, it's all 'that's DISGUSTING oh-my-God-I-don't-know-how-you-can-eat-that-crap'. She's like a badly-designed shower tap, running either way too hot, or incredibly freezing, with no in-between.

It was weird having Cheryl and Mum in the same room and I wasn't sure it was entirely wise. I did appreciate how difficult it must have been for them. I made a point of sitting with each of them and having a good old chat. It was nice to catch up with Cheryl. When I'd lived with her and Dad things got a bit weird and it seemed like she wanted me to be a miniature version of her. But now we live apart we get on very well and often speak on the phone when one of us is trying to track Dad down.

Whilst I had her there, I decided to pick her brains about what to wear on a hot date this season.

'Hot date?' she asked, grinning.

'Hmm,' I said, sniffing.

'I think I know who with,' she said. I looked at her closely. Cheryl is also friends with Portia and she hosted the barbeque where I bumped into Seth in the first place.

'Yes, I should think you probably do,' I said. I decided against telling her it was a double-date, or that it wasn't me who was interested in Seth. That would just get confusing.

'Leave it to me,' she said. 'When's the date?'

'Tomorrow.'

'OK, don't worry, I'll have it all sorted by then.'

I nodded. I knew she would too. Dressing me up was a kind of hobby with Cheryl.

I had a nice chat with Lance too.

'Have you moved in?' I asked. The question had been at the back of my mind for a few weeks and I'd decided it was time to settle it.

'Not officially, but yes,' he said.

'Oh I'm glad,' I replied. 'But you still have your flat, right?'

'That's right,' he said.

'Just in case,' I said.

'Just in case,' he confirmed.

Later I spoke to Mum.

'What were you speaking to Cheryl about?' she asked.

'Clothes,' I replied.

'OK,' she said. Mum, who'd basically invented the term 'charity-chic', had got used to the fact I was never going to talk to her about fashion. 'How's Al?' she asked.

I shrugged. 'Dunno. I haven't heard much from him since he ran off with some floozy.'

'Marina isn't a floozy,' Mum said.

I stared at her. 'How do you know about Marina?'

Now it was her turn to shrug. 'I talk to Al's mother.'

'What I'm not sure about,' I said, eying her suspiciously, 'is why no one told me about Marina before Al left. If it's all innocent and they're just friends, why all the secrecy?'

'I think Al and his mum might have been a bit worried about how you'd react to the idea of him going off on a six-week holiday with another pretty girl.'

'So she's pretty is she?'

'Yes, she's beautiful,' Mum said. Then, realizing her mistake, 'Er I mean no, she's not that pretty, just, er . . .'

'Easy?'

'No, she's, y'know . . .'

'Beautiful,' I said, scowling.

'Anyway,' Mum said. 'Doesn't sound like you're letting the grass grow under your feet, going out with Seth.'

'Great. Does everyone in Buckinghamshire know my business?' I asked.

'Only those who read your blog.'

'You're still reading the blog?'

'Er, no,' Mum lied. I knew she was of course. But it was easier to be in denial, otherwise I'd be censoring myself the whole time. I just smiled pleasantly.

'Must go and speak to Jugs,' I said, getting up and plumping myself down next to my friend, who was trying to stop Marley from sitting on her lap. I poured myself some wine.

'Get off her, Marley.'

He hopped off and went around to sit on Mum's lap instead.

'So,' I said. 'Did you actually see The Boy? I can't get hold of him. Think there's something wrong with his phone.'

'Yes, apparently he thought his phone was waterproof and dropped it into a pint of bitter to demonstrate,' she said. 'Turned out it was an entirely different model that was waterproof.'

'I see,' I said.

She went on. 'He came back to visit his mum last weekend and popped over for a cup of tea.'

'Tea?' I said in surprise. 'He drinks tea?'

'He was driving,' Jugs explained. 'He claims he doesn't drink and drive any more. He's only just got his licence back.'

'Maybe he *is* going straight,' I muttered. Don't go there,

Anya, I told myself.

'What's that?' Jugs asked.

'Nothing,' I said.

I watched Mum whisper something into Marley's ear, both of them glancing at me. Marley looked confused.

'What cake?' he asked loudly. Mum rolled her eyes and signalled to the waiter.

The cake was enormous and they made me blow all the candles out. And then cut the first slice. And everyone in the whole restaurant sang Happy Birthday and Marley drank some of Mum's champagne and he and Lance danced like Michael Flatley and I laughed till I nearly wet myself.

Dad handed me a few envelopes. 'These were on the doormat when we arrived,' he explained, 'and this one is from Cheryl and me.'

I opened the cards first, one from Mum with a modest iTunes voucher, one from Jake and Crumpet, one from each set of grandparents and one from Al, obviously written before he'd left and posted by his gran or someone as it was postmarked Allerton. Nothing from The Boy of course, but then again nothing was expected.

Afterwards we went back to Dad's flat and had hot chocolate and marshmallows. Marley went to sleep on the balcony. Mum cornered me.

'Darling, you know I've had to give up yoga?'

'Really?' I asked, shocked. Mum lives for yoga. 'Why's that?'

'I've got Benign Positional Vertigo.'

'What the hell's that?'

'It's when there's something wrong with your inner ear and it gives you the illusion of movement.'

'Like when Marley pretends to tidy his room?'

'It's actually quite unpleasant, Anya. Anyway, the point is I've got this new course I'm doing, only it's in Oxford and there's an induction tomorrow and—'

'Could you get to the point please, Mum?' I said, glancing at my watch.

'Is there any way you could babysit Marley tomorrow night?'

'You want me to make a three-hour round-trip on a Saturday so you can do one of your classes?'

'Yes,' Mum replied, flatly. 'There's a cheesecake in it for you.'

'What's Lance doing?'

'Saturday's his Rotary night.'

'Why don't you ask Cheryl to babysit?' I said. 'I've got tons of work to do,' I added, not entirely truthfully.

Mum thought for a bit. 'Look I've got an idea. Why don't I leave him here tonight? He can stay for the weekend. I'll give you some money to take him to the zoo.'

'But that means I have to take him back on Sunday.'

'You can just put him on the train from Marylebone, it's only half an hour, I'll collect him.'

'Mum! We can't send a seven-year-old on the train by himself.'

'Of course we can, he'll be fine. Just tell the guard to keep an eye on him, he'll love it.'

'Of course he'll love it, that's not the point,' I said. 'The point is he'll almost certainly lock himself in the automatic loo and they'll have to get the fire brigade out to free him. Have you forgotten the blast-door incident at the leisure centre?'

'Anya,' she sighed. 'You worry too much.'

'What is this course you're doing anyway? Hemp Appreciation? Advanced Tree-Hugging?'

'It's an exercise class actually,' she sniffed. 'It's all done sitting down so I won't lose my balance.'

'What's wrong with the aqua-aerobics you were doing down the leisure centre?' I asked, trying to keep a straight face.

'Oh they play such old music, I feel like I'm eighty. Why is it they assume that just because we're not in the first bloom of youth that we must want to be bombarded with Perry Como and Frank Sinatra? Do they think I listened to that crap when I was young? They should be playing Abba and the Rolling Stones.'

'You've got a point, I suppose,' I said, grudgingly, I used

198

to take Marley swimming while Mum did her class and had witnessed the poor dears trying to splash along to Val Doonican more times than I care to remember.

'Also,' I said, in support, 'Mrs Gorringe isn't perhaps as supple as you have a right to expect from a gym instructor.'

'Her boobs bash into her knees when she really gets going,' Mum agreed. 'I have no faith in her. So will you do it?'

'OK,' I said, secretly pleased to hear that Marley was going to be staying. As irritating as he can be at times, I do miss the little pest. Life's never dull with him around.

'Great,' she said, grinning. 'Phone me to tell me what train he's on, and make sure you sit him in the guard's carriage.'

Then it was time for Lance, Mum and Jugs to go. Cheryl and Dad were staying for the night as they'd both had a few drinks. Lance carried Marley into my room, then they went down to the car. It was only once they'd gone that I remembered that tomorrow night was the stupid double-date. How could I have forgotten that? What was I going to do with Marley? Oh well, there was time to sort that out tomorrow.

I checked my emails before I went to bed. Crumpet and Jake sent me an e-card and a five-pound Topshop voucher which was nice, but I was even more excited to receive this:

Email from Casper to Anya

Dear Anya

I'm so sorry. I feel terrible at what happened. Please don't hate me. It's taken me ages to work up the courage to write to you. I've started this email so many times and just deleted over and over again. The thing is, Anya. The thing is, I've not been entirely honest with you. I should never have agreed to go into London to meet you. It's just that you really seemed to want to meet me and I so didn't want to disappoint you and I genuinely wanted to go myself but, well, it was never going to happen really, and I should have known it.

I'm suffering from an illness you see. I have agoraphobia. A fear of open spaces. I can manage a quick trip down to the shops, or maybe a few turns around Brompton Cemetery, but really I was a fool to think I could go further.

I wrote more, but it seemed self-indulgent and whiny, so I deleted it. I'll leave it there but just ask if you could possibly find it in your heart to forgive me?

Well Anya, could you?

Yours humbly

Casper

Well, thank the Lord, I was starting to worry he'd slit his wrists or something. The investigation would almost certainly have fingered me as the culprit. I can see the headlines now: GENIUS AUTHOR HOUNDED TO DEATH BY TEEN EDITOR.

It was too late to respond, but I went to bed happy. Everything seems to be going my way for once, and as if to illustrate my point, just before I went to sleep, with my little brother snoring gently beside me, my phone buzzed and I checked it and it was The Boy, who'd evidently managed to get his phone working.

HAPPY BIRTHDAY LITTLE MISS UNDERSTANDING

LOVE

MR ME

Like I said, what a great birthday.

Email from Jack Stewart to all@Boxwood
Now my ruler's gone! Who's got my sodding ruler? I hate you people!
Jack

Miss Understanding Blog Entry
– 28th August 2010

I'm doing it again, aren't I? Going on and on about my own weird little life and ignoring your equally weird emails, which are, each and every one, little cries for help. So before I tell you what happened today, I must give you the results of the Top Five Things That Are Good About Being Single.

Saskia Garfield, (who, let's face it is only single in the loosest sense of the word) writes to tell me she likes not feeling tied down to just one man. I really hope you mean that in a metaphorical sense, Saskia.

Imogen Chivers likes to be able to snog anyone she likes. And frequently does, if my scout down at Allerton Rugby Club is to be believed. It gives a whole new meaning to the term Ruck and Maul.

Ben Noakes says he likes being able to eat the last Rolo.

Fat Gareth likes being able to eat all the other Rolos.

And finally, Jez Morton sums it all up for us by pointing out that the best thing about being single is never having to hear anyone say, 'You've forgotten what day it is, haven't you?'

Anyway, back to me . . .

I like Cheryl, as I think I may have mentioned before, but she can be a little irritating at times, like this morning when she yanked the sheets off my bed and left me in my T-shirt and knickers, spread out like a starfish. I quickly curled up in a ball, desperately trying to stay asleep.

'Well, that's the first thing to put on the list,' Cheryl said cheerily. She stood, looking fabulous even at this early hour, wearing four-inch heels, skinny as a WAG on an E. coli diet.

'What list?' I grumbled.

'The shopping list, I'm taking you shopping today.'

'And what's the first thing on this shopping list?'

'Bikini waxing strips.'

'Hey!' I said. Though to be fair, she had a point.

'Look,' I said, defensively. 'I'm not going to Ibiza this summer, who cares if the garden gets a little overgrown.'

'Who indeed?' she said archly.

'Certainly not Seth, if that's what you're thinking!' I said, aghast.

'That's between, you, Seth and your blog,' she said. 'Now get up and get dressed. We can eat in the lift.'

'Where's Marley?'

'Your dad took him to the Imperial War Museum, it's just us girls today.'

I looked up at her and sighed. I realized now asking her what to wear tonight might have been a tactical error. Oh, BTW, Cheryl's sorted out the Marley babysitting arrangement already. She's hired some expensive supernanny. Mum's OK with it. Marley's not going to know what's hit him.

Now, I've been to the massive underground shopping centre beneath Canary Wharf before, of course. But Cheryl has this uncanny ability to find shops you didn't know were even there. I think I must have an inbuilt, self-defence mechanism which kicks in when I pass a shop that's too pricey for me and which therefore renders it invisible. Perhaps such shops are invisible to everyone except those who possess the special key. Namely their stepmum's AMEX platinum card.

Cheryl thinks the point of wearing heels is to make as much noise as possible so that other shoppers get out of your way. And we needed a clear run. With Cheryl leading, we didn't just shop, we worked that shopping centre like Madonna works her glutes.

I tried on leggings and tights, skirts and wraps, bags and tiaras. We tried over-accessorizing, then just a simple necklace, we tried floral prints and hemp, we tried slingbacks and stilettos. All the time I couldn't help but think this was all a waste of time. It was obviously Cheryl's intention to hook me up with Seth. I know Seth likes me, maybe even fancies me a bit, but he is too sophisticated to go for someone as young as me. And besides, the object of the evening was for me to basically hurl Seth into Katie's arms and ride off with The Boy, or whichever Frankenstein Boyfriend Katie had assembled in her cellar. And besides, despite Al's absence and repeated lack of communication, I thought it slightly disloyal to be making such an effort over my appearance before going out with two other men. And while we're on the subject, for those of you who've written in to criticize me for 'seeing other blokes', as Jenna Hall put it, can I just remind you that I'm not seeing 'other blokes' or indeed anyone. This is a date for Katie, not for me. I'm just along for the free food and to see how long it takes Katie to 'accidentally' fall out of her top once she gets Seth on the dance floor.

Feeling slightly guilty at the extortionate amount of money Cheryl seemed prepared to waste on me, I did try to explain this to her but she was having none of it.

She stopped and swung me around as we stood in the checkout queue at Coast, where she'd selected me some sheer black tights and a lovely necklace I thought even Katie might rather approve of.

'Anya, let me explain something to you about men,' she began speaking quietly and intently. 'It's not your role to decide which of them you like and whether you're allowed to go out with this one or that one. Don't think that going out to dinner with an eligible young bachelor means that you're cheating on your boyfriend. You're not, unless you choose to invite said bachelor up for coffee when he drops you off at the end of the night. It's not your job to set boundaries. It's his job to find where they are. It's his job to pursue you if he wants to pursue you, your job is simply to look as beautiful as you can, and you, Anya, can look very beautiful indeed when you let yourself glow.'

'That kind of thinking opens up lots of doors,' I said as she turned to pay.

'Yes it does,' she said.

We had lunch in a posh café and Cheryl made the mistake of ordering me a glass of white wine. I got drunk immediately and started talking rubbish, as is my custom.

'So, do you follow your own advice?' I asked.

'What do you mean?' she asked absently, not looking up from the pile of receipts she was flicking through.

'Do you ever let men other than Dad test your boundaries?'

She looked up and smiled. 'Not any more,' she said.

'Why? Is there an age limit?' I asked.

'There comes a time in every woman's life,' she said, rather dramatically, 'when she has to stop messing about and accept the fact that she's going to be spending the rest of her life with the same man.'

'Surely that time is when you get married?' I suggested.

She shrugged. 'Actually, I think it's when you get pregnant.'

I looked back at her, then my eyes flicked over to the glass of cranberry juice she'd ordered.

'Not drinking today, Cheryl?' I asked.

She grinned.

'Babies need a lot of looking after,' I said.

She nodded, still smiling.

'But you quite like looking after people, don't you?'

'I really do,' she said, and grinned again.

So, tonight is the double-date. As suspected, The Boy has let me down and is not here. I phoned him this morning to thank him for his birthday text but I just got his voicemail as usual. I didn't leave a message, I'm tired of phone tag. So I gave Katie the go-ahead to bring in her stand-in. 'I have the perfect guy,' she said. 'He's your age and very sweet.' Yeah, whatever, Katie. 'Sweet' means 'shy minger' in this context.

Still, I was all up for it anyway, it's not as if my social

calendar is awhirl at present. I'm just looking forward to getting out of the house. I may even have a white wine spritzer. Though definitely not more than that for fear I'll come to at three in the morning with aforementioned spotty youth with his tongue in my ear and hand up my top.

That's all for today, except to ask if anyone knows anything about this Marina girl Al's gone on holiday with? Since Mum was going on about her at my birthday, I've been thinking about this. Why haven't I come across this girl before if she's such great mates with Al and family? I'm still a relative newcomer in Allerton, one of you busybodies must know her, spill the beans already!

Love munches

Miss Understanding

Miss Understanding Blog Entry
– 29th August 2010

Right, well it's tomorrow night now, and I'm still trying to get my head around the last twenty-four hours.

Here's what happened. Cheryl and Dad left around five, Dad sternly instructing me to do this and not do that, Cheryl winking and asking me if I'd changed the sheets. The supernanny came at seven-fifteen sharp. She's gorgeous. Irina's her name and she's all German with cheekbones as high as The Boy on New Year's Eve. Marley's jaw hit the floor when he saw her. I saw him glancing at the lockless bathroom door with a thoughtful expression. I showed her where everything was and she seemed satisfied as she said, 'Is good. Marley, show me how well you read,' before handing him a Roald Dahl book she'd thoughtfully brought with her. Marley seemed a little flustered as I left.

Seth came to pick me up at seven-thirty. We were

meeting the others in the lounge bar at the Clontarf, which is this flash boutique hotel in Old Street. I didn't want Seth coming up to the flat as, apart from Marley and Irina, it was wall-to-wall with laddered tights and inappropriate underwear, much of it Marley's. While I waited, Raj came out and said hello.

'Hey Miss Buxton,' he said.

'Hey Raj, I didn't see you this morning.'

'No, I had to go to the vet's,' he said, looking apologetic.

'Really? Everything OK?' I asked.

'I took my dog in for a check-up. It was very odd, the vet grabbed him by the ears and lifted him up off the floor.'

'Really?' I asked, puzzled. 'By the ears?'

'Yes. He says, "I'm sorry Raj, but I have to put him down." I said, "Why, is there something wrong with his ears?" "No," says the vet, "he's just really heavy."'

He boomed with laughter and I gave him a look.

'Oops, here's your man, I think,' Raj said. 'I'd better go before he gets jealous.' And he popped back inside as Seth swept up in his lovely big Jaguar. I hopped in quickly before he had the chance to jump out and open the door for me.

He grinned at me. He was wearing a casual suit and looked like he'd just stepped out of a Dolce and Gabbana ad. I felt pathetically grateful to Cheryl for helping me with my outfit.

'You look beautiful,' he said and I felt my legs suddenly go a bit wobbly. I had to physically restrain myself from tilting my head and giggling.

'Thanks,' I said firmly.

'Let's go,' he said. 'Cocktails await.'

As we pulled out into traffic he waved at the iPod in its neat little dock and asked me to put some music on. I wheeled through, most of the stuff I'd never even heard of. 'Who's Jethro Tull?' I asked.

'You wouldn't like it,' he said.

'Don't make assumptions,' I replied huffily, 'I might like it.' I played it and we listened in silence for a few minutes.

'What else have you got?' I said, wheeling through again. He chuckled at me. Eventually I found some Madonna and put that on.

'What's this?' he asked.

'Madonna.'

'I have Madonna?'

'Apparently.'

He thought for a bit as we headed in towards the towering blocks of the City.

'Oh yes. Ex-girlfriend residue I think. I need to purge.'

'Oh right, like when you go to the loo at your new boyfriend's place and you look in the cabinet and there's a tampon box there.'

He laughed. 'Yes, I suppose so. Madonna is the tampon box of my iPod.'

He drove quickly and seemed to know the roads well. We soon arrived at the hotel and he drove straight into the underground car park.

'How come you can park here?' I said. 'Isn't this just for guests?'

'I know a guy who knows a guy,' he said. I gave him a WTF look and he explained further as he swung into a reserved bay. 'We sometimes use this hotel for entertainments. You know, Christmas parties, bonus parties, that sort of thing. We have an understanding.'

'Well, get you,' I said. 'You know people who know people.'

He turned off the engine and we were plunged into sudden silence. He looked over at me, still smiling. Always smiling. I hadn't meant to be sneery. I was actually a bit impressed with him, with the whole package. I just didn't want him to know that. I often say dumb things at times like these. Before he could say anything weird, I opened the door. 'Let's go,' I shouted, my little voice echoing in the cavernous space.

Katie was wearing a tiny skirt and a clingy top showing off her boobs, yet she somehow managed to look quite classy, which was slightly annoying. She was already in the lounge bar when we arrived. I stopped dead when I saw who she was with. They were sitting on a couple of low couches with a coffee table between them. Katie . . . and Lucas. She'd only gone and brought bloody Lucas as my bloody date!

Katie stood and gave me a hug, whispering into my ear as she did so. 'I'm so sorry, the guy I had in mind pulled out at the last minute. I was desperate.'

'Why didn't you at least warn me?' I hissed back as Seth stood by awkwardly.

'Would you have come?' she asked.

'Of course not,' I replied.

'Well there you go. Seth, hello, this is Lucas. Lucas, this is Seth.'

Katie gave me a signal to sit next to Lucas, which I ignored and sat next to Seth instead.

'Hi Anya,' Lucas said.

'Lucas,' I replied stiffly.

'Can I get you a drink?' said a waiter suddenly standing next to me.

'Anya?' Seth asked.

'Yes please, I'll have a Tia Maria and Coke thanks. A double.' I said, feeling as though I might need it.

As it turned out, it wasn't as bad as I feared. Typically, the boys immediately started talking about football and

Katie and I chatted about people at work. Or at least she bitched about them, I nodded and did my non-committal shrug thing.

She didn't say anything about my dress. She didn't even sniff. Which I suppose is her way of saying she approves.

Conversation was a bit slow at first but Seth took command, telling us all about his forthcoming trip to Canada.

'Where the geese come from?' asked Katie, excitedly.

'Er, yes, though the geese we see here in London don't migrate here from Canada of course,' he said.

'No, of course not,' Katie said.

There was a pause.

'Anyone know anything else about Canada?' I asked.

After a drink, we went on to the Great Eastern, which is this three-floor bar restaurant in Hoxton, all black walls and stylish furniture draped with arty types and beautiful people. Lucas was behaving himself. As we walked along Old Street he fell in beside me. 'I'm really sorry about the other night, Anya,' he said. 'I'd had a little too much to drink. I shouldn't have tried to push Val like that.'

'You shouldn't have got into our taxi,' I pointed out.

'No,' he said. 'You're right. I feel ashamed of myself.'

In the restaurant, the boys discussed the wine list for ages, trying to outdo each other with how much they knew about wines. Katie pretended not to take any notice but was clearly loving it. I suppose from her self-obsessed perspective the men were competing for her attention. It couldn't possibly be that they were interested in the other girl at the table. They eventually settled on some expensive Italian red wine which was very nice, but not really any different to every other bottle of red wine I've ever tasted. I guess I'm missing something.

Ordering was difficult. I was anxious not to get anything on my dress, not because of the social embarrassment, but because Cheryl would skin me alive. I had to get something non-oily and without a sauce. Luckily Hoxton is the sort of place where the people are a bit high-maintenance about food, so I was able to get something called 'Organic Chèvre on Crostini'. Cheese on toast, basically. For twelve pounds fifty. Oh well. I wasn't paying, at least I hoped I wasn't. I was sort of assuming Seth would pay, or split with Lucas.

Conversation flowed smoothly. Katie was laughing like a drain at everything Seth said, even when he wasn't trying to be funny.

'So when Lehman Brothers went bust, my friend lost his house. And a week later he discovered his girlfriend was pregnant,' says Seth.

'Hahahaha,' says Katie.

Cue awkward silence. I stepped in to try and help.

'More wine, Katie?' I asked brightly, proffering the bottle.

'Can we have another?' Lucas called to the waiter.

'Good idea,' said Seth, his smile wavering for just a fraction. He cast me an amused look.

I chatted politely enough with Lucas, sitting to my right, all the time worried about how this was going to work. Assuming Katie could get Seth interested in her, and to be frank she was going to need more than a couple of bottles of wine and a shrieking laugh, what was I to do with Lucas? Would I have to make a show of flirting with him and avoiding Seth? Katie was obviously thinking the same thing. She stood. Seth followed suit and Lucas a split second later.

'I'm just popping to the Ladies, Anya,' she said glaring at me.

'OK,' I said.

She stood, waiting. The boys looked at me, wondering if they could sit down. 'Don't you need to go?' she asked.

'No I'm all right, Mum,' I said.

'Really?' she asked, giving me a look.

'My bladder is, at most, half-full,' I replied. 'I think I could probably even manage until I get home, as long as I don't drink too much water.'

'Anya!' she spat.

'OK, fine,' I said, 'I'll come.' I got up and followed her,

conscious of the boys smirking at each other.

'Can you start being a bit nicer to Lucas?' she said at the sinks, peering at her reflection and making minute adjustments to her hair.

'I thought I *was* being nicer to him,' I replied. 'I haven't kicked him in the balls, for example.'

'Look, Seth needs a clear signal that you're not interested in him.'

I thought about this. I had two problems. Firstly, I'd kind of changed my mind after a double Tia Maria and Coke and didn't feel totally sure I *wasn't* interested in Seth. Secondly, I really didn't like the idea of making any kind of signal that involved being in closer proximity to Lucas. I did find it interesting, though, that Katie had just revealed that she was of the opinion that Seth might be interested in *me*. Having said that, we did have a sort of agreement.

'I suppose I could give it a go,' I said, without enthusiasm. 'What sort of thing are you expecting from me?'

She'd obviously been thinking this over. 'Downstairs they have a club. We can go for a bit of a boogie. Just dance with Lucas and ignore Seth. You don't have to do anything other than dance.'

'Well, thanks very much,' I said. 'You sound like my pimp.'

'Anya, please try,' she pleaded, turning to me.

'*OK*, I said I would.'

When we got back to the table Seth asked me if I wanted a dessert.

'No!' said Katie.

'Yes, definitely,' I said. Katie rolled her eyes again.

'Is everything OK?' Seth asked her.

'Yes yes,' she said brightly. 'I'm just keen to get downstairs for a bit of a dance.'

'I can't dance without tiramisu,' I said, looking at the menu. Katie snorted.

'I don't think they do tiramisu here,' Lucas said.

'What! Who's heard of a restaurant that doesn't do tiramisu?'

'I agree,' Seth said. 'Ridiculous.'

'Totally,' I replied. 'What's not to love? Anyway, I suppose I'll have the ginger and chicory cake with frothed cherry jus. Whatever THAT is.'

Katie sighed and turned to Lucas. 'Lucas, did you know Anya is editing Casper Williams' new book?'

'Really?' Lucas said, looking at me with interest. 'You're editing the Bad Postman?'

'Why do you call him the Bad Postman,' Seth asked, walking right into it.

'Because he doesn't deliver!' Katie and Lucas finished in unison.

I groaned and sipped my wine, wishing I was somewhere else.

'Lucas designed the cover of the first book,' Katie said.

'What, the knobbly spaceship?' I asked.

'Yes, that's the one,' Lucas confirmed. 'Did you like it?'

'I liked the book, but since you ask I'm not sure I liked the cover. It would have put me off buying it.' The waiter brought my dessert and coffee for the others.

'We sold over eighty thousand in hardback with that cover,' Katie said breezily as I tucked in.

'Well, you might have sold eighty thousand and one with a different cover,' Seth joked.

'What would you know about it?' Lucas said coldly.

There was a moment where we all sat and wondered whether we'd just heard what we thought we'd heard. There was an edge of menace in Lucas's voice. Seth stared back at him equally.

'It was just a joke, mate,' he said calmly.

Lucas thought about responding but then seemed to think better of it. He nodded and turned back to me.

'Sorry you didn't like the cover, Anya. Next time I'll run it past you first, OK?' I smiled weakly.

'How's your dessert?' Seth asked, trying to steer the conversation away from cover designs.

'A bit too much ginger,' I said. 'And chicory.'

Later on, when I could avoid it no longer, we trooped downstairs, my heart sinking with every step. The downstairs area was uber-hip, with cushions and hard benches. It was filled with people wearing clothes I'd never seen before but instantly wanted to copy. Most people were drinking water, which seemed like a good idea. I'd drunk a little too much over dinner and had a raging thirst. I watched the Hoxton folk standing around casually and chatting comfortably despite the thumping beat of the trance music. How could they hear each other? Maybe they couldn't. Maybe they were watching one another mouth nonsense just for the look of it. Seth magically found us some large cushions and we nabbed ourselves a cosy corner while Katie popped off to the coat check to leave her handbag.

'Drink?' shouted Lucas into my ear as soon as I sat down.

'Water!' I shouted back.

After he'd gone to the bar, Seth leaned over. 'Do you like to dance?' I could see Katie mouthing 'no', shaking her head furiously and making throat-cutting gestures. It was almost as if she didn't want me to dance with him.

'Umm no, not really,' I lied.

He looked disappointed.

'Katie loves dancing though,' I said. 'Dance with her.'

Seth looked momentarily confused but nodded and

turned to Katie, who gratefully accepted his invitation. She winked at me as they went. I wasn't keen on being left alone and kept having to fight people off when they tried to pinch our cushions. I was actually quite glad to see Lucas return. He plonked everyone's drinks down and handed me a bottle. I drank deeply but slowly, trying to put off the inevitable. I could see him waiting. I finally had to put the bottle down when it was empty. Lucas grinned at me.

'Thirsty, huh?'

'Yeah, I guess.'

'Dance?' he said. I groaned inwardly.

'We'll lose our cushions,' I pointed out.

'Don't worry about the cushions,' he said and took my hand, pulling me up and onto the dance floor. I wanted desperately to snap my fingers and just be at home, back at the flat, or better yet, back in Allerton with Mum and Marley squabbling and Lance watching *Celebrity Come Dine With Me* in the sitting room. I saw Katie jiggling her space-hopper boobs in poor Seth's face. He shot me a wounded look and it was all I could do to give him a me-too shrug.

Once I was dancing it wasn't so bad. I closed my eyes and imagined I was dancing on my own. The tunes were good and I was a little tipsy and I got into the groove quickly enough. Then all of a sudden I felt Lucas up close and personal. I flicked open my eyes to find him leering at me and grinding his hips against mine. I rapidly tried to move back away from him but he grabbed my bum and squeezed, holding me to him.

Without thinking I shoved him and he tripped over someone's feet. I also went backwards, managed to keep my feet, but bumped someone's arm which just happened to be carrying a drink. Coke splashed across my new dress and started seeping through the flimsy layers to my skin. Instantly Seth was there asking if I was OK.

'Yeah, but he just grabbed my butt,' I shouted as Lucas stood up. Seth turned to face him. Katie looked furious.

'Sorry,' Lucas said, looking surprised. 'The way you were dancing I thought you wouldn't mind if I held you.'

'Is that how you hold someone?' I yelled. 'By jamming your fingers into their buttocks? I'm going to have bruises tomorrow.'

Lucas shrugged and wandered over to get his drink.

'He just grabbed you without warning?' Seth asked.

'Yes,' I said. 'But it doesn't matter . . . Let's just forget it.'

By now though the owner of the spilled drink had begun drunkenly remonstrating with Seth and my saviour had to turn to deal with that.

'Come on,' Katie said. 'Let's go to the Ladies and get you cleaned up.'

I wanted nothing more than to just walk out and jump

into a cab, but that would have been unfair on Seth. I went with Katie and she mopped me down.

'Sorry about that,' she said.

'It's not your fault,' I said sympathetically, before remembering that it actually *was* sort of her fault for bringing Lucas along in the first place. I took off the dress and stood in my bra and pants while Katie ran it under the cold tap.

Then my phone rang. I checked it, intending to turn it off, but when I saw the call was from The Boy I answered.

'Hi,' he said. 'So where am I meeting you?'

'What?'

'I'm in the car park under your building.'

'You idiot, you're three hours late. And why didn't you tell me you were coming?'

'I only just picked up your email,' he said hopelessly. 'I didn't get your texts, there's something wrong with my phone.'

'*You think?*'

'So where are you? I'll come and meet you.'

'I'm in Hoxton, but don't come here, I'm leaving soon,' I said, glaring at Katie, whose shoulders slumped as she finished rinsing off the Coke stains.

'What's that noise?' The Boy asked.

'That's my friend Katie drying my three-hundred-quid dress under the hand-dryer.'

'If she's drying your dress, then what are you wearing?' he asked.

'Virtually nothing,' I said, unable to resist. He made a sort of gulping noise.

'I'm coming,' he said.

'No don't,' I repeated. 'I've had an awful night. Because you didn't show up, Katie had to rope in some tosser who's been leering at me all night and just now started molesting me on the dance floor.'

'What?' he yelled. 'I'll kill the bas—'

'Just stay where you are, I'll be there in half an hour. Is the security guard there?'

'Um, yes, he keeps staring at me,' The Boy confirmed.

'Put him on,' I said.

There was a pause and some muffled voices, then: 'Hello?'

'Hi Raj, it's Anya.'

'Hey, Miss Buxton, how are you?'

'I've been better, but I'll be home soon. That shambolic mess you see in front of you is a friend of mine.'

'Really? He's wearing filthy plimsolls and a T-shirt that says Robot Monkey Love'.

'Yeah that's him, please let him into my flat, OK? He's sound. Ask him to keep an eye on Marley.'

'Are you sure? I was hoping I might be able to use my taser on him.'

'Let's just hold off on the taser for now, Raj.'

'OK, I'll take him up to your flat. He can keep that lovely babysitter company.'

'Wait!' I said. 'Actually, don't take him up there. It might . . . upset the equilibrium, as it were.' I didn't want to get home and find The Boy mauling Irina on the couch. 'Can he sit in the foyer to wait?'

'Hmmm,' Raj sounded doubtful.

'Tell him some jokes,' I suggested.

'All right then,' Raj said.

'Thanks, I'll see you soon, OK?'

'OK Miss Buxton, see you soon.'

I hung up, put my dress back on and prepared to face the music.

When we came back out Lucas was gone. I raised my eyebrows at Seth. He shrugged. 'We had a little chat,' he said, 'and your friend Lucas decided he needed an early night.' He's not my friend, I wanted to say. Katie stroked Seth's arm awkwardly and thanked him. 'Shall we stay for a couple more dances?' he suggested. I nodded and smiled. Now The Boy was in the foyer with Raj, I felt a little more comfortable.

We all danced together after that, though Katie kept shaking her bits at Seth. He didn't seem to be backing away too much, I thought. Maybe she was growing on him. Or maybe he was just distracted by her glittering boobs. I tried not to feel disappointed. Deep down I knew that I couldn't really compete with Katie. It's not that I'm undeveloped, just that, well I'm no Jordan. And she knew how to act with men. She didn't mind making an idiot of herself in order to get their attention. She knew how to make it clear she was interested in them . . . in that way.

I can't do that.

'Can I drop you home?' Seth said to Katie as we came out onto the street in the small hours. 'You're in Bethnal Green aren't you?'

Here we go, I thought.

'What about Anya?' Katie asked.

'Yes, I'm taking Anya back to her flat,' Seth said. 'But I'm happy to drop you off first.'

Yay! I thought, trying to look innocent as Katie shot me a filthy look.

'Well, I'm staying at Anya's tonight,' she said, thinking quickly.

'Are you?' I asked. 'Have we discussed this?'

'YES,' she said, glaring at me.

I shrugged. 'OK then.'

'Oh what a gorgeous car!' Katie purred as she saw the Jaguar. She called shotgun and waited for Seth to open the door for her. She moaned with pleasure as she sank into the leather seat. Seth closed the door and moved around to the driver's side, giving Katie five seconds in which to hiss at me, 'What are you doing? Will you back off?'

'I'm not doing anything,' I replied in a hurt tone. 'And will you stop having an orgasm in the front seat?'

Seth got in and handed his iPod to Katie. Hmph.

We pulled up outside the flat and Seth turned off the Norah Jones album Katie had selected. He rushed around and opened Katie's door. I sat in the back seat waiting for him to open mine.

'I had a lovely night,' Katie gushed.

'Well, I'm sorry about the unpleasantness with Lucas,' Seth said.

'You handled that really well,' she simpered.

There was a pause.

'It was nice meeting you,' Seth said. I peered out through the window. Katie was leaning towards him, boobs practically flopping out into the Docklands night. She was evidently hoping for a snog. Seth pecked her on the cheek. 'Goodnight,' he said and moved towards my door. Katie looked crushed. I suddenly felt a pang of sympathy for her. She'd done her best but it hadn't been enough. As Seth opened my door she backed off and moved towards the foyer, a hand raised up to her face.

I hopped out of the car, wanting to go after her. 'Thanks Seth, I had a really nice time,' I said glancing over at Katie.

'Me too,' he said.

'Night,' I said brightly and moved towards Katie. But Seth took my hand. Not roughly, but firmly enough to let me know he wanted me to stay for a little longer. I turned back to him, unsure of myself. Then I saw he wasn't smiling, and at that moment he was the most desirable man in the world. His eyes seemed to draw me in until I was transfixed. In the soft golden streetlights I could just see the beginnings of stubble making itself apparent on his strong chin. I found myself wondering how that stubble would feel against my cheek. Against my throat.

And then he was moving towards me and I wasn't moving away. And then his lips were on mine and mine stayed where they were and he was kissing me and I wasn't pulling back. I felt his hand on the small of my back and I felt like a starlet on the silver screen as I closed my eyes.

But there was something happening, something else. I heard footsteps, someone running and suddenly Seth released me and spun and there was a blur and a crack and suddenly Seth was on the pavement and standing over him, breathing heavily was a lank-haired and unshaven The Boy.

'Keep your hands to yourself,' my knight in not-so-shining Converse said.

Seth sat up and stared at him, rubbing his jaw in a daze.

'What the hell are you doing?' I hissed at The Boy.

He looked up at me, surprised. 'I'm saving you from the loser,' he explained.

'This isn't the loser,' I said. 'This is the *other* one.'

'What other one?' Seth asked, climbing to his feet and watching The Boy carefully.

'Never mind,' I said quickly.

'What, this is the one the other girl's supposed to be snogging?' The Boy asked, still confused.

'What,' began Seth, '. . . the hell is going on?'

I sighed and looked upwards. The game was up. Katie wandered back to join us along with Raj, grinning like a loon and waving his taser.

'Katie and I had this kind of arrangement,' I said. 'She likes you . . .'

'Anya!' Katie hissed.

'Oh for God's sake, Katie. I think he figured that out when you jammed your left boob in his ear during that new Peter Andre song.'

Seth blinked and waited for me to go on. I sighed. 'Look, Katie fancies you and thought that you and her might get to know each other if we had a double-date.'

'I see,' Seth said, moving his bruised jaw from side to side. 'So when you agreed to go out with me, it was so you could try and set me up with your friend?'

I winced. 'Well, when you say it like that it sounds a bit childish . . .' I ground to a halt. I wanted to tell him that I did like him too. And that I really liked the kiss. But I couldn't say that with everyone watching me. There was too much going on in my head, with The Boy standing watching me intently, and Katie in tears already and Seth now mad at me and Raj desperate to pump ten thousand volts into someone. I wasn't going to be able to fix anything tonight.

'OK Anya, I'm sorry. I got the wrong idea,' Seth said. He was smiling again. He turned to The Boy and held out his hand. 'No hard feelings?' The Boy looked at him in surprise, then shook his hand warmly, smiling back. How can men do things like that? Punch each other over a girl then suddenly agree to be one another's best man at the wedding?

Seth nodded at Raj, smiled briefly at Katie, then went to get back in his car. He gave me a strange, puzzled look just as he got in.

'I'll call you, OK?' I shouted. Well, I had to say something.

Then he got back in his car and drove off.

'Come on you lot,' I said, leading everyone inside. 'Let's

have some hot chocolate . . . Not you, Raj.'

Katie had rushed into the bedroom while I was showing Irina out and was now crying melodramatically. I gave The Boy a mysterious look. Mysterious because even *I* didn't know what it meant. I was very glad he was here on the one hand, and a little bit impressed by his Mr-Darcy-style life-saving act, but at the same time I was really pissed off with him for getting in the way again, just when things were starting to get interesting. Also, what would happen if Dad turns up unexpectedly tomorrow morning? They'd only met once before and that really didn't go well after Dad caught him feeding beer to the angel fish. 'Wait here,' I told him.

I went into the bedroom and handed Katie a tissue, then after reflection sat next to her and patted her back, resisting the urge to say, 'There, there.' She blew her nose.

Finally, I thought.

'These tissues are nice,' she croaked. 'Perfumed.'

I looked at the packet. 'They're free from animal testing too.'

'That's good,' she said.

There was a pause.

'Though if you *were* a lab animal,' I suggested, 'you'd probably want it to be tissues they were testing on you.'

'Yes,' she sniffed.

231

'Rather than have them put lipstick in your eyes, for example.'

She laughed briefly.

'I'm sorry about all that,' I said. 'I didn't know he was going to kiss me.'

She snorted. 'He was always going to choose you, that was obvious.'

I stared at her. 'What are you *on* about?'

'Oh come on, it was no contest.'

'I didn't get that impression at all.'

'OK, whatever, Barack.'

Now I laughed.

'I'm sorry I was rotten to you, Anya,' she said. 'You've been so nice to me.'

You haven't read what I've been saying about you on the blog, I thought.

Then a little voice disturbed us. 'What's going on? Who's that girl? And why is The Boy drinking Dad's whisky?'

'Sorry Marley,' I said, ushering him back to his room. 'I'd forgotten you were here.'

I managed to find beds for everyone. The Boy on the floor in Marley's room, which Marley loved. He's hero-worshipped him ever since he found out it was The Boy who tagged the bridge over the M40 with *There Were No Good Old Days*. I could hear my brother chattering away to him in the next room. Katie bunked in with me again. She was still sniffing, and I think they were sniffles because she was upset rather than her usual 'let's annoy Anya' sniffles.

'So are you going to go out with Seth then?' she asked after I'd turned off the light.

'What? Oh hell, I don't think so, Katie,' I replied. 'I don't think that would be a good idea.'

'Look,' she said. 'Don't refuse to go out with him on my account, OK?'

I was touched. 'Thanks, Katie,' I said. 'That's really nice of you, but I don't think Seth's right for me. And anyway, I'm not entirely sure . . .'

'Entirely sure about what?' she prompted as I paused.

'Well there's this guy . . .'

'The Boy.'

'No, I mean, yes, but The Boy's always there, causing trouble. Complicating matters. I mean another boy.'

'*How* many guys have you got on the go?' she asked, sitting up in bed. For the first time she actually seemed to be taking an interest in my life.

'I don't have *any* guys actually, currently on the go, as it were,' I said.

'Seth obviously fancies you,' she said. 'And The Boy, and so who's this other guy?'

'His name's Al,' I told her. 'He's supposedly my

boyfriend, I guess. Though that was never . . . official. He's in South America but I suspect he's seeing someone else and doesn't seem to want to talk to me right now.'

She paused for a while. 'I'm sorry Anya, I know how you feel.'

But I'm not sure Katie does understand how I feel. Because I'm not sure how I feel. Sorry, need to go and have a bit of a think in the bath.

Love

Anya

Email from Anya to Casper

Dear Casper

Even though you've stopped writing to me again, I'm going to assume you are reading your emails. I hope you'll respond, I also hope the writing goes well, but most of all I just hope that you're OK. I'm worried about you, Casper. Not worried about the book or your career, or the future of the company or even whether I'm going to look a fool at the next Editorial meeting, but worried about you.

Anyway, I thought I'd give you a quick update on my overly-complicated love life, more than anything because I need to write it all down to get it straight in my head. You're the only person I think I can trust with my feelings right now. There's Jugs, but, ever since she and The Boy had that thing, I can't really talk to her about that. Sorry if it's boring, but you did make the mistake of telling me you were interested, once.

It's Sunday night and I've finally got the flat back to myself. Marley has gone home to Allerton on the train, under strict instructions not to get locked in the toilet, or to reveal that I didn't take him to the zoo but instead to the pub with *persona non grata* The Boy, who I have only just now forced out of the flat using steely resolve and a roasting fork.

The Boy – why did I invite him down? It's not as if he's the ONLY guy who could have pretended to be my date.

This is what happened this morning, after Katie had drunk four pints of coffee and finally gone home. Marley was watching TV in the spare room and The Boy and I were in the kitchen. He'd filled a saucepan with Dad's fancy extra-virgin olive oil and was trying to fry some oven chips he'd found in the freezer.

'You can't have chips for breakfast,' I said. 'And you're supposed to cook these in the oven.' I noticed he'd got himself a jar of pesto from the cupboard as well.

He sighed and continued his intensive preparations.

'I'm surprised you even know what pesto is,' I said. 'You do know you can't smoke it?'

He pretended he couldn't hear me.

'And you're not supposed to deep-fry those,' I went on, pointing to the oven chips.

'Nothing wrong with deep-frying food,' he said, finally stung into responding.

'Yeah,' I said. 'Who wants to live till they're thirty?'

'Well, you know what they say, anything that doesn't kill you . . .'

'. . . just takes longer to kill you,' I finished.

'Look,' he said, 'now I live on my own, I can do things however I like. If I want chips and pesto for breakfast then I'll have them.'

'Yes, but this is MY flat and MY pesto,' I said, snatching up the green jar and holding it behind my back.

'Gimme that,' he said and grabbed for me. I shrieked and tried to run towards my bedroom, but immediately tripped over the rug and went down with a thump. In an instant he was on top of me and had grabbed my wrist.

I giggled with nervous excitement, not really sure what was happening here. He grinned and said. 'Let go of ze pesto,' in a stupid Mexican accent. Geography was never his best subject.

'Or else what?' I challenged. He wasn't pressing down on me with his full weight, but I was still breathless.

He considered for a minute. 'Or else I weel keess you.'

I paused a little too long before saying, 'No. Anything but that.' And he gave me a slightly curious look, perhaps wondering if he should pursue this. 'You can have the pesto,' I said, now wanting him off me, before . . . well, just before.

He got off and I stood quickly, brushing myself off and feeling awkward. Marley was peering at us interestedly over the back of the couch.

'Look,' I said, 'Marley and I are going to the zoo today. Don't make any mess.' Then we both looked at the kitchen already strewn with pots, pans and assorted cutlery. 'Clear up the mess you've already made,' I corrected, 'and make sure you're out of here by the time I get home. In fact make sure you're out by half-twelve because sometimes Dad comes back here on Sundays so he can get an early start. And I think he likes to go through my drawers looking for condoms.'

'Does he ever find any?' The Boy asked with fake casualness.

'None of your business,' I said.

'What's a condom?' Marley asked.

The Boy glanced around desperately. He spied Marley's pencil case on the table. 'Condoms are a type of . . . felt-tip pen,' he said.

'Brilliant,' I said, walking into the bathroom and shutting the door.

After a moment's consideration, I jammed a chair under the door handle, as they do in horror films. It wouldn't keep out a vampire perhaps, but at least The Boy would think twice before playing the whoops-I-didn't-realize-you-were-in-here trick.

After my shower we had a house meeting. Marley decided he didn't want to go to the zoo once I'd suggested I split the money Mum had given me with him instead. We wandered down to the river and had lunch together in a little pub, then went back to the flat for a lazy afternoon.

I knew I really should have asked The Boy to leave earlier. It was going to be hard enough keeping Marley quiet about the fact he'd been here at all. I couldn't let him stay too long. But if I'm honest I really loved it, the three of us there, like a little family, in our own place. I stretched out on the sofa and put my feet on The Boy's lap. He rubbed my arches and I snuggled under a blanket and watched *EastEnders*.

Marley was at the kitchen table working on an old Bratz colouring book he'd inherited from me. He was the first to break the silence. 'Where's the brown pen?' he asked. 'I need to do Courtney's bush.'

There was a brief pause.

'What the hell kind of colouring book is that?' The Boy asked, getting up to look. 'Oh, it's a *gardening* scene,' he said, peering over Marley's shoulder. 'I'd say that's more of a shrubbery than a bush. And you should use green, not brown.'

'It's winter,' Marley pointed out.

'Yes but you've lost the brown pen,' The Boy reminded him. Then he sat down to help. I watched them for a while, each concentrating so hard their tongues were sticking out a bit. How would it be? I found myself wondering, doing this for always.

'So what's this flat like?' I asked. 'In Doncaster.'

He looked up, a little guilty. 'Yeah, well about that. I kind of moved out.'

'Oh, did you find somewhere else?'

'Not exactly, I'm kind of between homes at present. I was hoping I could crash here with you for a while.'

'You did, huh? What about your job? Those Fray Bentos pies won't distribute themselves you know.'

'Yeah, well, that's the other thing I was meaning to talk to you about. There was a sort of . . . well, an incident.'

'An *incident*? Right, OK, go on.'

'I had a sort of race with one of the other drivers in the cold storage warehouse and I went a bit Lewis Hamilton going round a corner.'

'Oh God, did you hurt someone?'

'No, I just ran the forklift prongs into a refrigerated container full of prawn cocktails,' he said, sheepishly.

I laughed.

'It was terrible, Anya, such a mess,' he said, looking crestfallen at my lack of sympathy. 'It looked like the morning after round Kerry Katona's. They took my licence.'

'So what are you going to do now?' I asked. 'You can't stay here. Dad would kill me.'

He nodded. 'OK, well, I've got some mates in Hackney somewhere, I'll track them down. Sort something out.'

'You can't go back to Clifton? To your mum?'

He winced. 'Yeah I would, but it's just there was, well, there was this . . . *incident*.'

And at that point I realized he just wasn't going to change. The Boy couldn't be trusted. There would be no flat in Doncaster, there would be no pesto and oven-chip meals waiting for me when I got home, there would be no niece or nephew for Marley.

Actually, come to think about it I've had a lucky escape there. What a hellish existence I was fantasising about. What on earth was I thinking?

After I'd finally got The Boy out of the flat, I checked my emails and saw this:

Hi Lovely
I'm sorrysorrysorrysorrysorry.
I know it's been ages since I wrote but we've been in the jungle. Contrary to the impression you seem to have picked up, the South American rainforest is not jam-

packed with wi-fi hotspots. I've had to wait until we got back to 'so-called' civilization here in Puerto Carreño.

Are you sure I didn't tell you about Marina? She's the daughter of one of Mum's friends and they've met up with us out here. She's not local and certainly not bare-breasted. Or not that I've witnessed.

Anyway gotta go, Marina needs to use the PC and Dad's keen to get going. We're off to Venezuela tomorrow and there's a problem with the visas, apparently.

Yours

Al

Oh Casper, I don't have the bandwidth to deal with this. I can't think straight.

The IT guy at work showed me this function on my computer where you can defragment your hard drive and the computer organizes all the files into different coloured strips and slots them in neatly next to each other, clearing space. Yellow read-only files, green temporary files, blue compressed files. The empty bits are white. Beautiful, white empty space. Which you can then fill up with all sorts of new crap. Then start the process again.

I need to defragment my head. Maybe defragment my life.

Or maybe I just need to wipe the whole disk and start again . . .

Who knows? Hope to hear from you soon.

Love

Anya

Email from Edith to all@Boxwood – Monday 30th August 2010

Dear all

I think I may have turned up some evidence in the Case of the Missing Basket. I was in a meeting and I saw one of the cleaners walk past carrying about a hundred china cups in a deep white wire basket.

Could this be *your* basket, Giuseppe? I looked for the cleaner in question after the meeting but to no avail. I promise if I see her again I'll crash-tackle her and retrieve this essential piece of post delivery kit.

Regards

Edith

Email from Anya to Casper

Hi Casper

Don't be mad at me, but I know you're busy with the book and don't need distractions, so I've taken the (enormous) liberty of writing the synopsis for you. I appreciate that it's not going to be exactly as you've done it. But you told me your synopses generally don't bear any resemblance to the finished book, plus you've told me the essential parts of the story anyway.

So for your reference, I'm attaching the synopsis I'm passing to the Sales people. Obviously you don't have to follow this, you don't even have to read it, I'm sure it's no good, but I hadn't heard from you. Anyway I'll stop rambling now.

Best wishes

Anya

Synopsis attached

Email from Anya to Casper – after work

Dear Casper

Hope you're OK and you weren't too miffed about me writing the synopsis. Obviously you don't have to stick to it closely, or even at all. I just know the manuscript is going to be brilliant and once people read that the synopsis doesn't matter.

Things are fine with me. I really like it here, even though it seems so quiet now Marley's gone back to Allerton. His solo train journey passed without incident. It's wonderful having such a lovely place to live, I know most people my age aren't so lucky. I just turned off the lights and the telly and sat looking out over the sparkling city. I could hear this amazing, vibrant hum of the traffic, and the trains, and the planes, and the millions of mad people rushing about even at this late hour.

How mad are people in London? Well, take this example. The building opposite is a residential block and there's this one chap who leaves his blinds open all the time. He also walks around in nothing but a thong and a Native American headdress. I saw him come in one evening last week wearing a normal business suit, and later on that evening I saw him and he'd changed into his headdress again.

He doesn't do anything weird, no rain dances or anything, and I haven't seen him try to scalp the postman. He just potters about checking his email, cooking his dinner, watching telly. Just like me. Except he's in a thong and a headdress. And I'm wearing bright red leggings and one of The Boy's old T-Shirts that says *668 – The Neighbour of the Beast*.

Come to think of it, who am I to talk about fashion? I like Headdress Man.

Anyway, hope to hear from you soon.

Love

Anya

Miss Understanding Blog Entry
– 31st August 2010

Dad took me out for dinner tonight. Cheryl had told him I knew about the baby. I think he wanted to get to me before I got to Mum.

'I think it's great news,' I said, crunching a breadstick. I like to poke one end in my mouth then chomp really rapidly as I slowly push the stick in, trying to make it look like I'm swallowing it whole.

'Thanks Anya, that really means a—look can you stop that?' Dad said, frowning.

'Sorry,' I said and washed it down with a swig of apple juice.

'I'm over the moon about it,' he said, finally.

I looked at him carefully. Was he really? Mum had told me she thought he didn't want any more children.

'I'm pleased to hear it,' I said. 'I thought that maybe you . . . that perhaps it wasn't . . . what am I trying to say?'

'You wondered if I was too old?'

I shrugged and peered at my menu.

'I thought that too, Anya,' he said. 'I really didn't think this would happen. I didn't think Cheryl wanted a baby either, she told me she didn't.'

'So what happened?' I asked, watching him. He didn't look too old to be a new dad. He had a little beard again and was going through one of his youthful phases.

'People change,' he said. 'Situations change.' He took a sip of wine, thought for a while then went on. 'My life is stable now. Cheryl and I are stable. It just seems right, now, when maybe it didn't before.'

I nodded. I thought I understood.

'There's a lot to be said for stability,' I offered.

'Don't underestimate how important it is, Anya,' he said, looking back at me intently. 'Thrills and passion and racing hearts are all very well and good. But they don't last.'

I nodded. I think I knew that already.

Problem is thrills and passion are . . . well, they're thrilling and passionate, aren't they? Some boys make you feel safe. Some make your heart skip a beat. Settling down and playing safe is all well and good for crusties like Dad and Cheryl, but I'm too young for stability, aren't I?

Oh that's all for tonight. My head's in a whirl.

Love you all

Anya

Email from Seth to Anya

Hi Anya

Just a quick note to say sorry for the awkwardness I caused the other night. I totally misread the situation. I had a really great night and got a little carried away. Hope there's no hard feelings. I'm off to Canada tomorrow and will be back in the Autumn, I'll be visiting Mummy up in Clifton, so maybe we can catch up then?

Say hi to Katie for me won't you?

Best wishes

Seth

Email from Casper to Anya

My Dearest Anya

I'm so sorry for my long silence, believe me I've missed our correspondence terribly. Alone here in my little study it gets so lonely, and reading hilarious stories of your overly complicated social life is the only pleasure I get.

But work comes first and I've been trying hard to concentrate on my writing, with some results! I've been churning out the prose this last week and am at nearly eighty thousand words now. I expect to have the first draft to you a day ahead of schedule.

The only break from working I've had in the last few

days is when I had to take Davina to have her tubes tied, or whatever it is they do to cats to stop them having thousands of babies. There's been a tom hanging around recently sitting on the fence and singing like an *X Factor* reject. No matter how many tins of Tuscan three bean soup I hurl at him he won't give up.

I was lying in bed last night wondering where all this creativity has come from. After weeks, months and years of being blocked, finally the ideas are coming back to me, like sheepish children returning from the woods. I feel strong and in control again.

Do you know why, Anya? It's because of you. Because you didn't hound me, you didn't judge me. You believed in me and persevered. When I asked you to stop talking about the book and tell me about yourself, you had every right to tell me to mind my own business and sod off.

But you let me into your life and I thank you for that. My dedication in this book will be to you, my dear Anya.

Enough of this sentimentality. I'm desperate to know what's going on with all your various boyfriends. And what of Katie? At first I thought she was ghastly, but she's starting to grow on me.

Write soon

Love

Casper

Miss Understanding Blog Entry
– Wednesday 1st September 2010

Aha! So some of you DO know this Marina. I'm getting mixed reports.

'She's a bitch,' says the possibly biased Erica Bainbridge. 'She told my boyfriend's sister about how I got thrown out of Allerton Water Park after I got caught snogging Daz Hall in the toddlers' pool.'

'I know Marina,' writes Saskia Garfield, more sympathetically. 'She lives in Girton. She's lovely. Al and Marina go way back, I'm surprised he hasn't mentioned her to you before, really. Frankly Anya, I suspect your worst fears may be true. After all, while the cat's away and that. Just look at you.'

Well whaddya mean just look at me? I am so totally *not* playing while that cat is away. I thought I'd made this clear. Sheesh!

Seriously though. Let's just say, for the sake of

argument, that Al *isn't* fooling around with Marina the Sex Kitten. Does me going out on dates constitute infidelity? I know what Miss Understanding would say about it, so don't anyone try quoting stuff I've written back at me. Just tell me what you think, OK?

I can't believe I received an email from Seth, apologizing to *me* for *his* behaviour. How does that work? I'm the one who should be apologizing to him (though I hadn't actually got around to doing so, now you come to mention it). These days it seems everyone spends their whole time trying to come up with reasons why things aren't their fault and making nonpologies. It's refreshing to find someone who apologizes for things he hasn't done.

On to work. I'm so relieved to hear Casper is actually working on his book and hasn't gone quiet because he's dead, or lost the use of his fingers or something. Having told Claire something good was on its way I feel like my ass is on the line too. I know I'm back to school next week but I don't want to leave a ginormous steaming pile of crap behind me when I leave. I was a bit concerned that Casper didn't mention the synopsis I did for him, but I'm going to let that drop. God knows what goes on in famous writers' minds, but I'm sure he doesn't want me banging on about minor issues like that.

Claire came in late this morning, she looked a bit rough. I popped my head around her door.

'Are you OK?' I asked, concerned.

'Just a tiny hangover,' she said, shuddering with the effort of speaking. 'Could you get me a coffee please?'

'Coffee's not good for headaches,' I said gently. 'It's a diuretic you see.'

'Don't give me any of that Scientology crap,' she said. 'Get me a double-strength ibuprofen and a triple espresso.'

When I brought back the coffee I told her about Casper saying how he could deliver by the due date. I figured she could do with some good news.

She looked up at me, eyes suddenly bright, if still slightly bloodshot.

'Are you sure?' she asked, 'What did he say, exactly?'

'He said he'd done eighty thousand words.'

Claire bashed her fist on the table causing me to jump and her plastic coffee cup to splash out over the pile of manuscripts in her in-tray.

'That's fantastic,' she said. 'This is going to be huge.'

'That's if the book's any good,' I suggested quietly, not really wanting to wee on her chips, but feeling I had to at least raise the possibility.

She paused, then said, 'Can't you get him to show you some of it?'

'He won't. He says he wants to get it right before he sends it in.'

Claire thought for a while, then shrugged. 'If it's good, then that's a bonus. People will buy it just because it has his name on it.'

'But if it's rubbish no one will want to buy his next book.'

'That's not our problem, Anya,' Claire replied, tipping coffee off the manuscripts into the bin. 'We're certainly never publishing another book with Casper again, far too much trouble. We'll just be happy to recoup the advance.'

I nodded at this. It seemed a little harsh, to be honest. Poor old Casper had just needed some support, after all. I didn't say anything. Claire looked up at me.

'Anya, I don't know what you did,' she said, 'but if this book comes in on time, as it now looks like it might, then we owe you, big time.'

Not sure exactly what she's suggesting, but it certainly can't hurt my future job prospects I suppose.

L8rs

Anya

Email from Anya to Casper

Hi Casper

Thanks so much for your email. I'm really pleased the writing's coming along again. I can't wait to see the first draft. I've mentioned the imminent delivery to Claire and she's really excited, we all are. Katie's fine, by the way, thanks for asking.

You asked me about my 'boyfriends'.

Well, as it stands at the moment, I don't really consider that I have a boyfriend at all, and quite frankly I prefer it that way. I'm a little confused myself to be honest, so let's just muse over the current list of men I know.

Al – missing in action. Last seen consoling a lusty exotic temptress on a sun-kissed beach somewhere in the tropics.

The Boy – now also missing in action. Thought to be dossing on the louse-infested settee of his friend Bonkers Garth somewhere in Hackney Wick.

Seth – now in Canada according to Portia, Vancouver to be exact. Still considered to be unsuitable boyfriend material due to age and also likelihood of having a pre-existing string of extremely attractive, rich and potentially violent girlfriends. His feelings for me are still unclear, particular after ex-boyfriend punched him in the face.

Lucas – evil beast-man who could be much improved by chemical castration followed by a good slap.

Anyway I think that's about all for now? Unless you know of any other eligible young men I should be adding to the muse list?

Yours

Anya

Email from Casper to Anya

Dear Anya,

Taking a quick breather from the writing. I know it seems strange to stop writing a novel and instead write an email to you, but this doesn't feel like work. It doesn't even feel like writing. Quite frankly chatting to you through the ether is the only proper social intercourse I have these days, unless you count asking Mrs Gupta at the newsagent on Lilly Rd if the new copy of *Empire* is in yet. She just says. 'What?' Her English is nearly as bad as her hearing.

Actually, come to think of it, I need your advice, I'm thinking of having one of the characters in the book say 'There are two types of people in the world X-People and Y-People.' And then go on to explain who's what and why. But the problem is I can't think what the two types of people should be. What do you think about this?

There are three types of people in the world; those who can count and those who can't.

Just kidding. Try this.

There are *two* types of people in this world. Dog people and Cat people. And I don't mean people who like dogs and people who like cats, I mean people who act like dogs and people who act like cats. Dog people are warm and enthusiastic and faintly ridiculous. Cat people are clever and self-interested and sophisticated.

Simon Cowell is a Cat person. Ant and Dec are Dog people. Barack Obama is a Cat person. Gordon Brown is a Dog person. David Walliams is a Cat, Matt Lucas is a Dog. Do you follow?

Anyway, I am a Cat person who wishes he were a Dog person. I get the impression you are a Dog person who pretends to be a Cat person. Am I right with any of this?

Yours

Casper

Email from Anya to Casper

Dear Casper

I'm not sure about being a Cat person or a Dog person. I see myself more as a Goat person, constantly bleating out the same plaintive cry 'Where's the freaking manuscript, Casper?' I bleat three or four times a day. And my bleating goes unanswered.

What are your thoughts?

Anya

Miss Understanding Blog Entry
– Thursday 2nd September 2010

I quite like Casper's 'There are two types of people in the world' concept. Why not write in and give me your ideas. I'll kick off with this one; there are two types of people in the world: those who've seen Kelly Binns' boobs, and those who haven't. I shudder when I remember that I'm in the former group after the incident with the paddling pool at Kayleigh Leach's summer party.

This whole Casper's-gonna-deliver-his-manuscript thing is getting out of hand. The PR department has been hauled out of the wine bar and told to put together a plan of action. We had a meeting about it today. The PR Director's name is Peter Fisher but everyone just calls him PR Pete. We all crammed into the meeting room to hear his pitch.

'Right,' he said, clapping his hands together like a school teacher. He has a totally irritating voice, he sounds like a cross between Mr Bean and Alan Carr. 'We're very excited about this new book from Casper Williams, and we're going to make a big splash about it. We've already started production on some giveaways, we're going to get the cover design and Casper's name on literally *everything*. Cups, mouse-mats, T-shirts, baseball caps, you name it.'

'Tube posters?' Claire asked.

'Er no, not Tube posters, the budget wouldn't cover it,' he said.

'Key-rings?'

'Yes, we will have key-rings,' he confirmed.

'Condoms?' asked David from Design.

'Wha—? . . . condoms? No of course not condoms. Look, can we move on please?'

He talked a lot about 'going forward'. As in 'We'll roll out these new synergies going forward.' Or 'We'll check the figures monthly going forward.' Well, you could hardly do these things going backwards, I felt like saying.

All the time we were in there I was worried about what I was going to say to Claire if Casper doesn't deliver.

He has to deliver. He has to.

Love

Anya

PS I've decided not to publish the results of the straw poll on whether I'm being unfaithful to Al by going out with Seth AS A FRIEND! Because you've all obviously missed the point. By the way, Bubbles Gosling, there is only one 'z' in Jezebel.

Thanks.

Email from Casper to Anya

Hi Anya

I'm going to tell you about my ex-girlfriend, Sarah. Lovely girl and very stylish. Too stylish in fact, if I'm to be brutally honest. You know how some people are always at the cutting edge of fashion? Well, she was a few months in advance of the cutting edge of fashion. You know how the first time you see someone wearing a new style, you think, 'What's that idiot wearing?', and it's only the third or fourth time you see the look that you think you might consider wearing it yourself.

Well, anyway she was ALWAYS that person. Only thing was, by the time everyone else got around to wearing the new look she'd have long since moved onto something equally outré. In other words, she was ALWAYS the person everyone pointed and laughed at. Sometimes it's nice not to be pointed at.

Went to the pub last night. It was OK but there were some dodgy blokes hanging about wearing beanies and sunglasses like the Fonejacker, so I came home. I really need to get myself some friends. I think I'm going a bit funny.

How are you getting on?
Love
Casper

Email from Anya to Casper
Hi Casper
Nice to hear from you and all, but really I think now you
need to concentrate on the book? Plenty of time for
emailing once you've delivered. Sorry if that sounds a bit
mean, but I'm under a lot of pressure here to get a book
out of you.
Anya

Email from Casper to Anya
Dear Anya
Don't worry your pretty little head about it.

Just finished a marathon stint working on the book.
four thousand words today. Just sat down this morning
and started writing. Next thing I knew, five hours had
gone past. I would have gone on but Davina broke the
spell by jumping onto the keyboard, mewing with hunger
and obviously concerned for my sanity. So I thought I
needed to take a break. Fixed some food for Davina,
made myself a cup of tea and some toast (have you tried
Gentlemen's Relish? It's a sort of anchovy paste and is
completely delicious on hot toast, I live off the stuff) and

sat down to read your latest blog. So nice to hear from you. I'm sorry to hear about all your uncertainties with your various men; cads and gents alike, so obviously enraptured by your charm, wit and beauty. You're lovely enough just on email. I'm certain had I met you for lunch the other week I too would have fallen for you head over heels and you'd have yet another gibbering idiot following you about mournfully.

Men are like buses, you wait ages for the right one and when it arrives you realize you've left your Oyster card in your other coat and can't get on after all. (Note to sub-editor: This metaphor may need some work.)

At times like this I find it helps to hear horror stories of other people's tragic love affairs, it makes you feel smug by comparison. Take heart from the story of my break-up with Sarah for example. The thing about Sarah, you understand, is that although she's a completely lovely, warm, kind and funny person, she's also utterly mad. She believed in aliens, angels, shadowy government conspiracies – you name it. She thought the *X-Files* movie was a documentary. Also, she was a terribly nervous person, and worried all the time. Not about her appearance, but about her job, her mother, about whether she'd left the iron on and of course about our relationship. She obsessed over dates and birthdays and things, like did she have time to get so-and-so's card to them in time? Did she have presents for everyone who was likely to get her one at Christmas? Was she going to give a present to someone who hadn't got her one? Would they feel bad about it? That sort of thing. Her personal organizer was in three volumes and had a contents page and a bibliography.

Anyway, the date she dumped me was kind of significant. It was February the thirteenth. Could have been worse, you might think. Could have been the fourteenth – Valentine's Day. But you might rethink when I tell you the thirteenth is my birthday.

'Why?' I sobbed. 'And why are you doing this to me on my birthday? How can you be so cold?'

Sarah shrugged, fighting back tears herself. 'That's part of the problem,' she said. 'You have a birthday so close to Valentine's Day. Don't you understand what kind of pressure that puts me under? I have to worry about making *both* days special, not just one.'

'The fact that someone has an inconveniently-timed birthday isn't sufficient reason to dump them,' I tried to tell her.

'I know,' she cried. 'But this year the thirteenth is a Friday and that's just the final straw.'

So that was a little disappointing. She went out with a Leo after that and I heard they got married and the next year she had a child. But get this, the baby was born on their wedding anniversary. The poor girl couldn't handle it and last I heard she'd taken to drink.

So let that be a lesson to you, Anya. I'm not really sure exactly what lesson, mind you, but learn from it, I urge you.

OK, must get on.

Love

Casper

Email from Anya to Casper

Dear Casper

Sarah sounds like an, um . . . interesting person. I had a friend at school who was a bit of a conspiracy theorist. People believe in all sorts of rubbish these days, don't they? Angels, homeopathy, capitalism, you name it. Have you considered using her as a character in one of your novels? Maybe you already have?

Yours

Anya

PS I know what you're doing BTW, Williams. You're trying to distract me from asking about your book. I'm on to you.

Miss Understanding Blog Entry
– 2nd September, supplemental

Hmph. Claire has just pulled me aside and asked me if Katie had mentioned to me whether I'd like to do some work for them as a freelance proofreader.

'Yes, she did. It was really nice of her to think of me,' I replied.

'Nice?' Claire said, puzzled. 'I *told* her to offer you some work. It's not a question of being nice. You're good at checking proofs and we need reliable readers.'

So when I thought Katie was doing me a favour, she was in fact just carrying out Claire's instructions. The cunning little cow.

OK, I asked you for your best 'There Are Two Types of People . . .' suggestions. Can't say I was inundated, but I think I can scrape together five good ones.

Dan Boyle thinks there are people who like reality TV, and those who don't. That's fair enough, Dan, but I find myself in both categories at once. They don't call it car crash TV for nothing. Hey, there's an idea for a new reality TV show, *Celebrity Police, Camera, Action!*, where Timmy Mallet and Saskia from *Big Brother 7* drive to crash sites in an emergency vehicle, giving first-on-scene medical attention and trying to direct traffic.

Our resident Neanderthal Guy DuLancey thinks there are two types of people: Men and Women/Gays. Well thanks for your unreconstructed input, Guy. We've missed you.

Jenna Hall says the two types are Cyclists and Motorists. Pedestrians don't count, apparently. 'Pedestrians are just motorists in between vehicles,' she says, enigmatically.

Sonia Bailey says there are Lovers and Fighters. Which I kind of like, really. It's a sort of Roundheads and Cavaliers, or Romance and Enlightenment. It reminds me of that Jackson-McCartney duet, *The Girl Is Mine*, where Michael Jackson says 'I'm a lover, not a fighter.' Yeah, we knew that already, Jacko.

Rollergirl takes the biscuit this week though, with, 'There are two types of people, Dancers and Drinkers.' That one speaks for itself. Personally, I'm a dancer, especially after a few drinks . . . eh?

Love yas

Miss Understanding

Email from Anya to Casper

Hi Casper

I've bolloxed it all up. I just got this email from Al:

Anya

What the hell is going on? I go away for a few weeks and happen to mention there's a someone of the female persuasion in the same country and you go mental. What's all this about 'putting things on hold'? You know I don't read your blog (reading what you do write on it is difficult enough, imagining all the things you *don't* put on is far worse), but you might be interested to know that my sister does, and now we're back in Bogotá she's been catching up and she's told me all about you going on a date with this Seth guy. Honestly, Anya, he's like five years older than you.

I really like you, Anya, and I know you 'don't want to go too fast', and 'you aren't sure if you know what you want' and all that standard girl crap but I thought, when you kissed me at the airport that that meant something. I've been really looking forward to getting back and seeing you. But now I don't know what to think.

My flight is BA102 from Bogotá, it gets in at 3.20 pm on Friday 3rd September. It would be nice to see you there, but . . . well, that's up to you.

I probably won't have time to check my emails again

before the flight leaves.

I guess I'll see you at Heathrow.

Or not.

Al

Now I don't know what to do. Should I go and meet him? That's tomorrow. I'm supposed to be at work then. I can't just waltz off to Heathrow, but if I don't I guess that's it for me and Al. He sounds pretty mad, and I guess he has the right.

Oh I wish you'd email me and let me know how you're getting on.

Yours

Anya

Email from Jack to all@Boxwood

Dear all

OK, who's had my stapler? It's a special extra long one and it has *Jack, Production* written on the top in Tippex. I urgently need it for stapling the costing report for tomorrow's meeting. If I find who keeps pinching my stuff I'll staple your damn hands to the desk.

Jack

Miss Understanding Blog Entry
– 3rd September 2010

I've had some pretty weird and wonderful days so far in my short life. There was the time my mum crashed my dad's car into a lamp post, the time I crashed my stepmum's car into a fence post, the time my car crash of a relationship with The Boy ended. The time my *second* car crash of a relationship with The Boy ended (that's a story for another time).

Actually, just reading that back I realized that those were all bad days, whereas this one was . . . oh let me just tell you what happened.

I got to work this morning hoping against hope that there might be an email from Casper with his manuscript attached. No such luck. He needs to deliver by Monday morning.

Claire came out and asked me if I had it in and I lied to her. 'Casper's just putting the finishing touches to it,' I said. 'It will be with you on Monday.'

'Wonderful,' she said. 'I'm so pleased with the work you've done for us this summer, Anya.'

'I've really enjoyed it,' I replied, feeling horrible.

'I hope you'll remember us when you've finished college,' she replied.

I smiled and nodded. If Casper doesn't deliver, as I am guessing he won't, I rather think that neither of us will forget this little episode.

'Ooh get you,' Katie said when Claire had gone.

'What?' I asked sharply, in no mood for her barbed comments.

'You'll be Editor of the Month next.'

'What's wrong with that?' I snapped. 'Just because I take pride in my work . . .' but I held myself back rather than say something nasty. Mum would have been proud.

She shrugged. 'It's just that I thought you said you wanted to be a writer, that's all.'

'So? Are you going to tell me I can't?'

'You can be an editor, or a writer,' she said. 'But you can't be both.'

Here we go again, I thought. 'Bollocks,' I said. 'I can do anything I want.'

She didn't say anything, just watched me.

I turned to my keyboard and started furiously hammering out another badgering email but then stopped myself. What would Ugly Betty do in this situation, I thought. Would she email the recalcitrant Daniel Meade? Would she send him a letter? Text him? No, she'd do none of these things. She'd go and see him, wake him up, send his floozy packing, make him some coffee and get him back to the office to do battle with the evil Wilhelmina. OK, maybe I took the Ugly Betty analogy too far, but I'd made up my mind. I went in to see Claire.

'Casper wants to meet with me,' I lied again. 'He wants to discuss a few last-minute things with the manuscript.'

'OK,' she said. 'Take a taxi, you can claim it back on expenses.'

'Thanks.' Then on an afterthought, 'Oh I also might need to go to the airport.'

'The airport?'

'There's someone . . .' I stopped, choked up for a moment.

'Is it important?' she asked, seeing my face.

I nodded, trying not to cry.

'Take as much time as you need,' she said.

I love Claire.

As I swept out, Katie asked me where I was going, but I just ignored her.

Twenty minutes later I was in Fulham. The black cab I'd hailed crawled down the car-lined residential road as I read out house numbers. Huge, Victorian terraces cast an autumnal shadow over us.

'One hundred and forty-one,' I said, excitedly. I had almost expected it not to be there. For so long Casper had been such an insubstantial figure. Did he really exist? I paid the driver and he took off, leaving me alone in the quiet street. I looked up at the house. 141 looked like all the other houses on the street. Perhaps slightly more shabby. The front garden was just weeds and wheelie bins. I walked up the path and rang the bell, my heart beating nervously.

I waited for an age but there was no answer. I banged on the door, wondering if the bell was broken, but this produced no response either. I tried to peer through the glass but it was frosted, so I crouched down and peered through the letterbox. I could see a hallway and a flight of stairs, both with Seventies patterned carpets. A grubby, tasselled lampshade hung at an angle from the hall light. The house looked like it had been warm and comfortable thirty years ago but had been left to sink into squalor. This was the house of a reclusive writer all right. Or perhaps an old man with no more family left to hold the other end of the new wallpaper roll.

I peered in through the front bay window. The living room was empty, just an old dusty sofa, a leather armchair and about a thousand books, in teetering piles on the floor.

I went back to the door, banged on it again and pressed the bell. But still there was no answer. I sniffed, blinked and found I had tears running down my cheeks. It couldn't end like this, could it? I stood there on the doorstep, crying. Suddenly all the stress, the worry and the tension of the last few weeks came bubbling out of me. The business with Lucas, Seth and The Boy, Katie's two-faces, Dad being annoyed at me, my confusion over what Al was up to in Colombia, and worst of all, most difficult of all, the breakdown in my communication with Casper. I'd thought that if I could just get the manuscript out of him then this summer wouldn't be a total write-off.

And now he's not even here. Eventually I pulled myself together. There was nothing for it but to go back to the office and tell Claire what a mess I'd made of it all. Then I'd get on a train to Heathrow and try to patch things up with Al. Then go home and just put this all behind me. Mum would understand. I'd tried my best.

I heard footsteps behind me, someone walking down the street, and I paused to let whoever it was go by, not wanting them to see my tears.

But the footsteps didn't walk on by. They stopped. Right behind me. And I heard a voice say 'Anya?'

I turned around. And there was Casper, nonchalantly smoking a cigarette.

Once I'd dried my tears and Casper had ushered me into the house, I felt a bit embarrassed about being caught blubbing like a child on his doorstep. 'I was only at the shop on the corner,' he explained.

I overcompensated by bustling around the house, opening blinds, doing the washing-up and tidying away the piles of magazines and books on Casper's kitchen table. He just sat and watched me, with a curious expression on his thin face.

He looked just like the publicity photos I'd seen of him, though he was better-looking in the flesh, and much thinner.

'You look pale,' I said. 'Have you been eating?'

He shrugged. 'I had some toast.'

I looked in the fridge, most things in there were covered in mould. I think some at the back had grown legs and started their own civilization.

'I'll make some tea,' I said. I hadn't entirely got the hysteria out of my system and needed to keep myself busy.

'Do you have any milk?' I asked.

'No,' he said. He was sitting calmly at the kitchen table smoking his cigarette and watching me flutter about.

I turned to him. 'But you just went to the shop?'

'Ah yes,' he said. He pointed to a notebook on the

272

table. 'I was sitting down to write a little shopping list when I realized I needed some ciggies. I can't write anything without nicotine, so I popped down to the shop to get some so I could write the list.'

He leaned forward, picked up the pen and wrote *MILK* at the top of the page.

'Wait here,' I said and ran down the street to the shop on the corner. I was back in five minutes with milk, bacon and eggs. Casper beamed enthusiastically when he saw this.

'My favourite,' he said.

I turned on the stove and it exploded.

'Oh, best not use that,' Casper said. 'There's something wrong with it.'

'You think?' I said. I looked about. There was a microwave. Thank God for Home Ec. You can cook bacon and eggs in a microwave. Casper looked on with growing respect as I prepared breakfast.

'Eat,' I said, plonking a plateful of food in front of him.

He looked back at me. 'You haven't asked me about the manuscript yet.'

'No,' I said, sipping my tea. 'Not till you've eaten, that's more important.'

'OK, Mum,' he said, smiling. He wolfed the food down like Johnny Vegas on a pre-diet binge.

'Now give me a look at this manuscript,' I said once it

was all gone.

'There isn't one,' he said. 'I haven't written it.'

I slumped down on the table. 'Oh Casper,' I said, though I'd known all along he was going to say that. After a minute I lifted my head to see him looking back apologetically.

'But you told me you were well into it,' I whined. 'What happened?'

'I lied,' Casper said. 'I never really wrote anything.' He laughed, but then stopped when he saw my face.

'Why not?' I asked.

'Because I can't,' he said. He sat back in his chair, pulled the packet of cigarettes out of his top pocket and proceeded to light another. The acrid scent caused my nose to twitch and I instinctively thought of The Boy.

'What do you mean, you can't?' I asked. 'You're saying you have writer's block?'

But he was shaking his head. 'No, I mean I can't write. I'm not a writer, Anya.'

'What are you talking about?' I said. '*Ask Me No Questions* was brilliant. I mean that. Everyone thinks so, not just me.'

'Ah,' he said. He took a drag of his cigarette and blew the smoke to one side, presumably having noticed my look of distaste. 'The thing is, I didn't write that either.'

I stared at him for what seemed like an age, trying to

work out what he was talking about. He helped me out.

'It's got my name on the cover, but I didn't write it.'

'Then who did?'

'My grandfather,' he said. 'His name was Casper too.'

I stood up and walked to the sink to pour myself a glass of water. He continued, now speaking to my back.

'He wrote it years ago. When my parents died I came to live here, with him. I was young and had these dumb ideas about being a writer. I used to keep a diary, trying to put down all these terrible, sad feelings I had. I thought if I could lock them up into words and shut them away in my diary, I could escape from myself. It didn't work of course, but my grandfather encouraged me. I suppose he was pleased to see me doing something rather than just lying on my bed crying.'

I sipped the water and listened. A clock ticked somewhere in the empty house, counting away the seconds, reminding me that there was a deadline here, for all of us.

'He took me up into the attic,' Casper went on, 'and opened a dusty old trunk. He handed me a yellowing manuscript and asked me if I'd like to read it. That was *Ask Me No Questions*.'

'But that book's about spaceships and things, it isn't the book of an old man,' I said, feeling ridiculous for saying it. Why was I arguing?

'He wrote it during the war,' Casper said. 'When he was a young man.'

'Did he not send it to a publisher?'

'He thought it was rubbish,' Casper said blowing smoke up into the air above me, where it swirled around beneath the high, nicotine-stained ceiling. 'When I read it I realized it wasn't. I persuaded him to let me type it out on Dad's old computer.'

'And you sent it to Boxwood?'

'That's right,' he said. 'After the old man died. I didn't see the harm at that point. I thought it would be a fitting legacy for him. He was a good man.'

I turned around and glared at him. 'And when they accepted the book? Did you not think it might be a good idea to tell them you weren't the author?' I asked.

He winced and looked guilty. 'The problem was they were only interested in a two-book deal. They offered so much money.' He fixed me with a pleading look. 'I needed it. I'd lost my parents and my grandfather, I didn't have anyone.'

I sat down. Casper sniffled and wiped at his left eye.

'You don't think I felt guilty? Well, I did,' he laughed bitterly. 'I convinced myself I wasn't *technically* lying when I said I wrote it because I typed the book out. I also made some of the language more modern, and introduced the nanobots. They didn't have nanobots in Gramps' day.'

'So you thought you could just write any old rubbish for the second novel and get it published?' I said.

He nodded.

'And the best you could come up with was *Tree Hospital*?'

He smiled. 'Well that was a joke, really. Claire was doing my head in demanding the next book. I just sent in loads of stupid ideas, hoping they'd give up eventually. But then they pointed out that if I didn't deliver I'd have to return half the advance.'

'Which I'm guessing you've spent already?' I volunteered.

He held up a packet of cigarettes. 'Tobacco doesn't grow on trees you know.'

I glared at him. 'This isn't funny.'

'Sorry,' he said. 'I was going to own up a few weeks ago, but then you turned up and started writing to me. You were so sweet, and lovely and enthusiastic. For a while there, when I was tapping away at the PC, sending rambling emails to you, and reading your insane blog, I almost believed I was a writer. I liked it, I liked the feeling.'

'Of course you did,' I said.

'But you are what you are,' Casper said. 'I am what I am.'

'I'm not sure I agree,' I replied. 'You are what you

277

decide to be.'

'Well, I've decided I'm not a writer,' he said.

'Then RE-decide,' I replied. 'Like they say. There are two types of people in the world, writers and editors, and you're definitely a writer.'

'But I can't write,' he pointed out.

'You *can* write,' I replied softly. 'You write beautifully.'

He just stared back, doubtfully.

'Your emails, they're so well-written. You have a lovely turn of phrase and a good ear for dialogue. I love reading your random ramblings.' I sipped my tea and stared him down. 'Not just the ones you sent to me, but all those ones you sent to Claire, before I started. Your correspondence with her is hilarious.'

Casper shrugged. 'But what good are emails? I'm supposed to be writing a novel.'

'Well, yes, there is that,' I agreed.

'It's hopeless,' he said.

'What are we going to do?' I moaned. 'We're going to be in such trouble.'

'It's not *your* fault,' he said. 'I'm the one who'll get sued for the advance money.'

'But I told Claire you were just about to deliver. I lied to her.'

'Why did you do that?' he asked.

'Because I believed you!' I shouted. He looked surprised.

'Did you?' he asked.

'Yes. I believed *in* you,' I said. 'I trusted you, I thought we had a . . . a connection.'

'A connection?' he said. 'You make me sound like the Rain Man.'

I put my head in my hands and let out a strangled cry.

'What about Davina the cat?' I asked. 'Is she made up too?'

''Fraid so,' he said.

I stood up and wandered around the kitchen. Come on Anya, I thought. Use your noggin. You're supposed to be clever. What would Ugly Betty do? No hold on, what would Miss Understanding do?

Then I had it. The brainwave. I turned around to look at him, thoughtfully. Could he do it?

'Why not a novel made up of emails?' I suggested. I hadn't thought this through properly yet but the idea was starting to take shape. 'Not just emails, but letters, your stupid synopses, your correspondence with Claire, with me.' I paced around the room, getting more and more excited as the ideas came. 'Hey, you can even use some of my blog entries,' I said. 'We'll change the names and things, but this could work, there's enough material there for a book.'

Casper said nothing, he just looked back at me. Was he thinking? Was he waiting for me to say something else?

But then, finally, he spoke.

'I suppose it could work,' Casper said, slowly. 'But I don't have time to write it, even if I knew what I was doing. The deadline is Monday.'

'I can help,' I said. 'I'm sure we can do this if we work together,' I knew I sounded a bit like Stephanie from *Lazy Town*, but I didn't care.

He was sitting looking out the window, deep in thought. 'It can't just be a book about people emailing each other. It needs a plot, it needs to go somewhere.'

He paused for a while, thinking. I waited.

'It's a book about writing a book,' he said finally. I could see his face change as it all clicked into place. He grabbed the notebook and started scribbling.

'See,' I said. 'You *are* a writer.'

He ignored me. 'OK, there's this young editor, a bit wet behind the ears . . .'

'Hey,' I said.

'. . . and beautiful,' he continued.

'With good cheekbones,' I added, nodding.

'Yes,' he said, peering at me. 'And very thin eyebrows.'

'OK! So maybe I went a little overboard when I finally got around to the big pluck.'

He continued. 'And so this girl starts up a correspondence with a difficult author.'

'Who's a bit odd,' I said.

'But quite sweet really,' he said.

'Yes. I suppose,' I replied. 'But mostly just odd.'

'And he's stuck for ideas, but the editor helps him. She shows him how to break his writer's block . . .'

'She gets the contributors on her blog to come up with ideas for books,' I added.

'Yes, they work out the plot together . . .'

'She has to write the synopsis,' I said, bitterly.

'Then he goes quiet on her . . .'

'She goes to see him . . .'

'He admits he hasn't written anything . . .'

'They come up with an idea together . . .'

'A book about writing a book . . .'

He began scribbling again.

'This is making my head hurt,' I said. 'I'm going to make a sandwich.'

When I turned around, Casper was gone. I heard the tapping of a keyboard coming from above and wandered up the stairs, munching my sarnie. Casper was in a little box room at the front of the house, where a tiny wooden desk was set up next to a single bed. He didn't look up as I came in. His cigarette burned in a filthy ashtray. I walked over to the window and looked out into the street.

'Hey, that's not your car, is it?' I asked. 'The Jaguar?'

'Hmmm? Yes it is,' he replied absently. 'It was my father's.'

'It's beautiful,' I told him.

'I suppose so,' he said.

'When I've gone back to school,' I said, another idea forming. 'You're going to need a new editor.'

'Not Claire!' he said, in alarm.

'No,' I said. 'Not Claire. I have someone else in mind. Someone who might like a ride in that Jaguar of yours.'

He said nothing, just went back to tapping the keys and scraping the mouse. I watched him work, his face burning with energy. I'd done that. I'd made that happen. I'd got him moving, got him working. And for the first time since my initial email to him, weeks ago, I finally felt confident in him. And maybe I felt some confidence in me, too.

'Hey,' he said. 'Do they get together at the end?'

'Who?' I asked.

'The editor and the writer?'

I thought this over. 'I think it would be more powerful if the relationship remained platonic.'

'Perhaps a little flirtation?' he suggested, looking up at me with an unreadable expression.

'Yes,' I replied. 'That might work.'

'But ultimately any suggestion of romance should remain unresolved,' he said. 'That's right.'

I stood and watched him for a while. He was cutting and pasting email correspondence into a new document.

'I'll tidy this up later,' he said, 'and write links to fill in the gaps.'

'OK,' I said. 'Obviously we won't expect it to be polished, but if you could deliver a good solid chunk on Monday, with a detailed synopsis, then that should be enough to keep Claire happy.'

'And prevent me from getting sued,' he said.

And prevent me from looking like a prize prat, I thought.

'You're sure I can use bits from your blog?' he asked. 'I'll change the names of course.'

'Actually don't bother,' I replied. 'I've already changed them.'

'Great,' he said. 'That'll save time.'

'Can I get you anything?'

'Coffee,' he said. 'Make me a pot of coffee. And could you clean out this ashtray, please?'

'OK,' I said, watching him in fascination.

Then he stopped typing. 'Hang on,' he said. 'Don't you have somewhere to be?'

I raised an eyebrow.

'Heathrow?'

I shrugged. 'I don't know. After the way I've treated Al this summer, I'm really not sure I'd be welcome.'

'He said he wanted to see you. To talk to you.'

'He'll see me at school.'

Casper looked at me. 'I think if you waited until you saw him at school it might be too late, yes?'

I shrugged. Then nodded.

'I think it would be nice if you were there, when he gets off the plane, don't you?' he said.

'Do you do relationship counselling in your spare time?'

He frowned at me.

'I don't know,' I said. 'I've been wondering whether I shouldn't take the opportunity to give up on poor old Al.'

He said nothing, waited for me to go on.

'It's just I'm not sure if he's the right one for me. Whether he's . . . what I'm looking for.'

'What *are* you looking for?'

'Oh I don't know,' I said, peering out the window. 'I'm just not sure I feel excited about him, do you know what I mean?'

'No.'

'I mean he doesn't make my heart skip, like . . .'

'The Boy?'

'No.'

'How do you feel when you think you might lose Al?'

I pretended to think, but I already knew.

'Sad.'

'Just sad?'

'And scared,' I said, surprising myself.

'So Al doesn't make your heart skip a beat when you see him, because he's safe.'

'I suppose.'

'But when you feel that safety might be taken away, lo and behold, your heartbeat starts skipping all over the place?'

I looked at him and nodded.

'Well, there you go then,' he said, as though everything was sorted now.

'OK, fine,' I said. 'I'll go to the airport.'

'Great,' he said, and turned back to the computer.

'Are you sure you don't want me to stick around and help you out?' I asked.

He shook his head. 'No, this is my job. You've done enough already. It's time for me to get this done.' He turned back to his monitor and started tapping again. 'I'll call you if I need any advice.'

I let myself out and stood in the street to call the office. I told Claire I was going to Heathrow after all. She was fine with it.

'How's Casper and the manuscript?' she asked, a little breathlessly I thought.

'Fine,' I said, 'It's not entirely finished, but it's going to be pretty good.'

'Really?' she said, as if she hadn't believed this would be my answer. I reminded myself that Claire knew Casper a whole lot better than I did.

'Yes,' I replied. 'I'm not worried about it. Not any more.'

Al and family were just about the last to come through customs. First I saw Mr Al swatting at one of Al's little sisters who had clambered up onto the luggage trolley and was trying to open a pink carry-on bag. Then I saw Al's mother, who spotted me straight away and I *think* looked pleased to see me. I waved. Al came out next and I was surprised to find my heart do a little fluttery jump. His mother tapped him on the shoulder and pointed me out. He stood for a moment, perhaps trying to read my face, before waving tentatively. Then Al's little sister slipped and knocked all the luggage off the trolley. I heard Mr Al yell, 'For the love of f . . .' before he managed to restrain himself and the Al family all bent to pick up the fallen bags.

My phone rang. It was Casper. I didn't want to answer but it looked like Al would be busy for a couple of minutes so I took the call.

'Hey Anya,' Casper said. 'Where are you?'

'Heathrow,' I replied. 'What can I do for you?'

Then another family came out, one of them a young girl. I realized this was Marina. She was exactly what I'd imagined, all long brown limbs, big firm boobs and light brown hair. To my delight Al ignored her and said something to his mum, she nodded and took over Al's trolley. He waved again and trotted past the waiting drivers and their handwritten signs. Towards me.

Casper's voice crackled from my little phone. 'So how should this book end?' he asked, as a tanned and fit-looking Al walked up to me, smiling tentatively.

'It ends the same way it began,' I said. 'With a kiss . . .'

And I snapped the phone shut, unable to stop grinning like an idiot. What happened next I'm afraid to say, Dear Readers, is between me and Al.

Email from Katie to Anya – Monday 13th December 2010

Hi Babe

I promised you some more work . . . I hope you're not too busy now you're back at school, because this is a big one. It's Casper's manuscript, only four years late. (I'm posting it to you as I know you don't have a decent printer.) As Claire pointed out at the Editorial meeting last week it wouldn't have arrived at all if it wasn't for you.

Anya, it's good. It's really good. Completely different style and genre to his previous book. No science fiction. It's this sort of post-modern romance all told in email and blog form. It's very self-referential and I have this strange feeling as I'm reading that he's writing about me. I mean,

I think the editor character in the book might be based on me. Does that sound weird? I think it must be just my head playing tricks. I'm bound to think like that I suppose considering how close Casper and I have become over the last few since he asked to have me as his new editor.

Now you mustn't tell anyone this, Anya, as it's a total no-no, but he's taken me out to dinner a few times. On Saturday he took me for a drive in his Jaguar, it's so nice. Not as new as Seth's but there's something about those classic S-types. He's not exactly loaded, but he does own a house in Fulham and if this book does as well as we think it's going to then his future's pretty bright. Plus he's rather dishy, as I think you must have noticed.

Best not get carried away dreaming of wedding dresses though. He is still a little odd, and anyway, I'm rather enjoying work these days so am in no hurry to get hitched and spend the rest of my life organizing gymkhanas and doing charity work. Portia's been ever so nice to me lately and I get a lot more respect at the Sales meetings. I think some of your ballsiness rubbed off on me you know, Anya? I do miss you.

Anyway, must get on. Have a meeting with the abominable Lucas later to discuss the cover for Casper's book. If he tries to put a knobbly spaceship on it again I shall rip his tonsils out and thrash him with them.

Love

Katie

PS Don't suppose you know anything about the dedication, do you? Casper wants it to read as follows:

To Miss Understanding, to whom I owe everything.

Sarra Manning

NOBODY'S GIRL

Bea thinks she's the most boring seventeen-year-old in the world. She's not pretty or popular or funny, unlike her mother who had Bea when she was 17. The only glamorous thing about Bea is the French father who left before she was born and lives in Paris. She yearns for la vie Parisienne every moment of her dull existence.

So when Ruby Davies, the leader of her school's most elite clique picks Bea as her new best friend and asks her to go on holiday with them, she's wary but delighted. If nothing else it's two weeks away from her over-protective mother. But when the gang arrive in Spain, Bea is crushed to realise that Ruby and her posse have simply been using her

978 0 340 88373 0 £5.99 PB
MAR 2010

http://sarramanning.blogspot.com
www.twitter/sarramanning

Also by Sarra Manning

let's get lost

ome girls are born to be bad ... Isabel is one of them. Her
iends are terrified of her, her teachers can't get through
her... her family doesn't understand her. And that's just
e way she likes it. See, when no one can get near you, no
one will know what keeps you awake at night, what
ou're afraid of, what has broken your heart ... But then
Isabel meets the enigmatic Smith, who can see right
hrough her act. Bit by bit he chips away at her armour,
nd though she fights hard to keep hold of her cool, and
er secrets, Isabel's falling for him, and coming apart at
the seams when she does.

Sarra Manning

let's get lost

978 0 340 87701 2

Also by Sarra Manning

Pretty Things

Set against a backdrop of North London and drama group, four unforgettable teens struggle for identity, self-esteem and some kind of significance in life in this wittily, wickedly observed comedy of teen manners!

Brie is in love with Lancome Juicy Tubes, Louis Vuitton accessories and Charlie, her gay best friend. But Charlie is in love with 1960's pop art, 1980's teen movies ... and serial heartbreaker, Walker. Walker has only ever been in love with his VW Bug, until he meets Daisy. And Daisy is far too busy hating everyone to know what love is ... This is a story about kissing people you shouldn't, falling in love and off your heels, and breaking hearts because there's nothing to watch on telly.

978 0 340 88372 3

Also by Sarra Manning

guitar girl

Seventeen-year-old Molly's band was always just about being a girl, singing Hello Kitty Speedboat and pretending to play instruments with her best mates Jane and Tara. But then the arrogant Dean and his sidekick T hijack the band and suddenly the fluffy girl band becomes *The Hormones* - a real band with a record deal - and they're heading for the big time. Molly slips further and further away from her old life and straight into a tangled love-hate relationship with Dean. Then there are the constant parties, the drugs and the phonies who pretend to like you when they don't ... Molly is living her dream, and she's never felt lonelier in her life. But has she got the strength to walk away from the band, and start again?

978 0 340 86071 7

Diary of a SNOB

Diary of a SNOB — *Poor little Rich Girl* — Grace Dent

978 0 340 98974 6 £5.99 PB
OUT NOW!

Diary of a SNOB — *Money can't buy me love* — Grace Dent

978 0 340 98975 3 £5.99 PB
MAR 2010

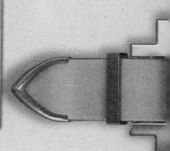

ALSO BY GRACE DENT:
Diary of a Chav

Book 1: TRAINERS V. TIARAS

Book 2: SLINGING THE BLING

Book 3: TOO COOL FOR SCHOOL

Book 4: LOST IN IBIZA

Book 5: FAME AND FORTUNE

Book 6: KEEPING IT REAL

www.bebo.com/poppetmontaguejones
www.shirazbaileywood.co.uk

VAMPIRE DIARIES

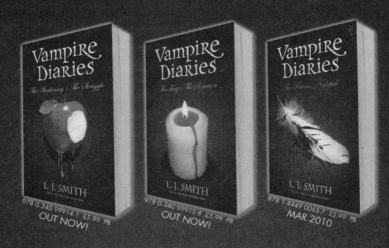

Vampire Diaries
The Awakening · The Struggle
L. J. SMITH
978 0 340 99914 1 £5.99 PB
OUT NOW!

Vampire Diaries
The Fury · The Reunion
L. J. SMITH
978 0 340 99915 8 £5.99 PB
OUT NOW!

Vampire Diaries
The Return: Nightfall
L. J. SMITH
978 1 4449 0063 7 £5.99 PB
MAR 2010

During the time of the Italian Renaissance, brothers, Damon and Stefan Salvatore fell in love with a beautiful young vampire named Katherine. Though Katherine's heart was big enough for both brothers, each of them vied to make her his own. The battle for Katherine's affection led to her eventually death, and left the two boys immortal, heartbroken, and forever quarreling.

Soon to become a major new ITV series

L. J. SMITH

The *New York Times* Bestselling Author